HOW TO
BECOME KING

HOW TO BECOME KING

Jan Terlouw

Hastings House, Publishers
New York

Published in the United States of America in 1977 by Hastings House, Publishers, Inc.

Copyright © 1971 Lemniscaat Rotterdam. Originally published in the Netherlands as *Koning van Katoren*.

Published in Great Britain in 1976 by Blackie and Son Limited.

Library of Congress Cataloging in Publication Data

Terlouw, Jan.
    How to become king.

    SUMMARY: Seventeen years after the king of Katoren dies, a boy aspires to win the crown and is tested with seven impossible tasks by seven Ministers.
    [1. Kings and rulers—Fiction]   I. Title.
PZ7.T268Ho   [Fic]   77-12471
ISBN 0-8038-3039-4

Printed in the United States of America

Contents

Prologue

Seventeen years ago there was a wild and stormy night in the country of Katoren. It was a particularly important night for two people: for the old King of Katoren and for a new-born baby by the name of Stark.

It was the last night of the old King's life. He was eighty years old, and he had grown very tired of sitting on his throne. He had always been a friendly, easy-going sort of man, blessed with a lucky streak that stayed with him to the very end.

"When I die," he used to say, "I hope it is a nasty, wet, stormy night full of hail and snow and thunder and lightning—because I would hate to die on a warm spring night that smelt of flowers. On a night like that I would want to wander in my park and look at the swans in the lake and set off wonderful fireworks: I wouldn't want to die!"

And sure enough, his wish was granted. On the night he closed his eyes for ever, the worst storm of the century struck Wiss, his capital city. The tempest lifted the King's spirit from the old, withered body and carried it far beyond the lands of the living.

The last night of the King's life was also the first night of life for baby Stark. He was born when the storm was at its height, at the very instant that an enormous thunderclap exploded over the city. He was born with his eyes wide open.

"It's a boy!" announced the midwife, "and his eyes are blue!"

It was lucky for Stark that the only things he cared about that night were drinking milk and sleeping. He was blissfully unaware of the terrible blows that fate was about to deal him.

Stark's father was a bricklayer, working on the restoration of the great Cathedral of St Aloysius. Early on the morning after Stark's birth, a messenger came from the Palace with the news of

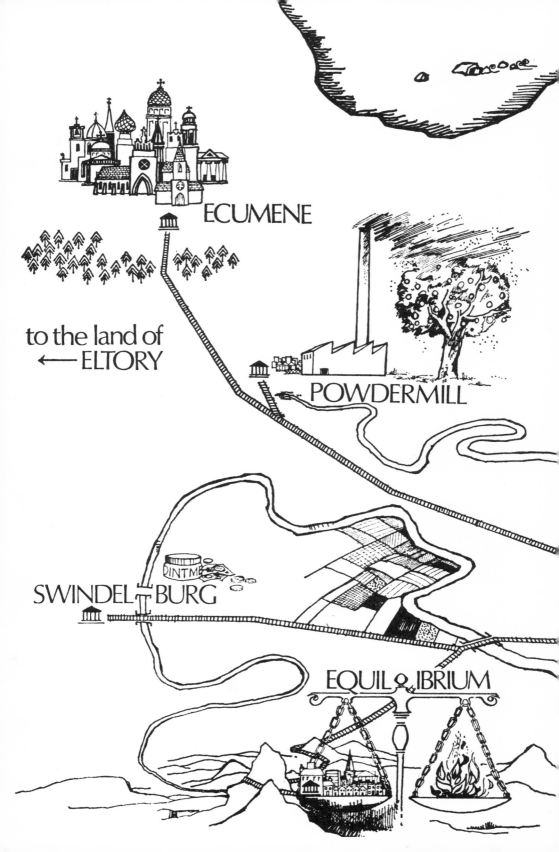

ECUMENE

to the land of
← ELTORY

POWDERMILL

SWINDEL–BURG

EQUIL♀IBRIUM

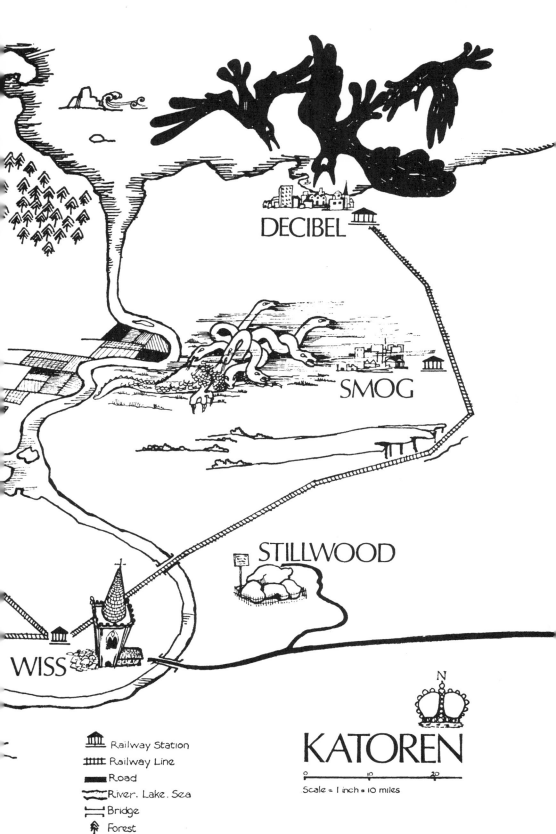

DECIBEL

SMOG

STILLWOOD

WISS

N

KATOREN

Scale = 1 inch = 10 miles

Railway Station
Railway Line
Road
River. Lake. Sea
Bridge
Forest

the old King's death. Would the bricklayer be so good as to climb the Cathedral tower and hang the flag at half mast? Stark's father had been up the whole of the previous night, of course, on account of his new-born son, and his mind was not on his work. He missed his footing and fell from the top of the tower. When they brought the terrible news to Stark's mother, she collapsed in a state of shock, and died a few days later. So baby Stark was now an orphan.

The old King had no children, and no one in Katoren knew who would succeed to the throne. As is usual in such circumstances, there was a lot of squabbling and intrigue. Finally six of the dead King's Ministers seized power, formed a temporary coalition government, and promised to work out a plan to find a new king. They declared that Katoren should have an excellent king, the best of all possible kings, they guaranteed . . . and so on and so forth. Before very long, of course, these Ministers were as stuck to their supposedly temporary positions as a nose to a face, and they and they alone ruled Katoren.

But the people of Katoren continued to mourn their old King. He had reigned over them for fifty years and they had loved him. He had not believed in ceremony, he did not make long speeches, and had often walked and talked with his people in the streets. And, like everyone in Katoren, he had loved fireworks. He had made a law that at least three times a year there were to be great fireworks displays throughout the land—on his birthday, on New Year's Eve, and on at least one other occasion, for which there was no set day. Whenever the King felt like it, the radio simply announced early in the morning that it was a King's Day. Everybody was to have a holiday, with fireworks in the evening. But all that was now in the past. The Ministers had banned all fireworks from Katoren.

Of course, baby Stark knew nothing about dead kings or dead parents, or living Ministers. He was a sturdy, curly-haired child with a strong chin. When he was hungry he yelled at the top of his voice until his Uncle Gervaas heard him. Uncle Gervaas was Stark's father's elder brother. The day the King died and Stark became an orphan he had thought long and hard about the meaning of life. For thirty-three years he had been the Palace butler. He had polished the silver buckles on the King's shoes, brushed the King's coat, and called for the King's coachman. Now, in the space of just a few days, he had lost his beloved King, and his dear brother and sister-in-law. He was sitting wondering what purpose there was in his own life now, when he heard Stark crying for food. So Gervaas got hold of a bottle and teat and some milk and fed his little nephew as best he could. He took the boy home to his little house at the back of the Palace garden, and there Stark grew up.

The old man kept his job, for the Ministers used the Palace for their conferences. All his life Gervaas had handed hats, talked respectfully, and made himself invisible. He disliked being subservient, but he couldn't change the way he had been brought up. So he decided to educate his little nephew differently. When he grew up Stark would not be obsequious, but forthright and confident, speaking his mind boldly. So the little boy got scolded only when he did not dare speak up for himself, and otherwise he could do as he pleased.

The years passed and still the Ministers did not name a successor to the King. People no longer believed that there ever would be a new King. Then one night Gervaas had a dream—a remarkable dream. He dreamed that he was lying back in a deep chair next to the King's throne. Someone had filled his pipe for him, and beautiful young girls were wafting cool air towards him with golden fans. Looking round, he could see that someone was sitting on the throne. Had the old King come back, or was this the new one? He craned his head further round, and, lo and behold, to his great amusement it was his own nephew, Stark.

Gervaas thought and thought about the meaning of his dream. The boy had been born on the awful night the old King had died. He seemed to be courageous, intelligent, and honest. The more Gervaas thought about it, the more he became convinced that Stark should be the next King of Katoren.

I

How to Become King

The oldest Minister is called Sure. He is about sixty years old, and the deep wrinkles on his forehead give his face a careworn expression. He never smiles. On his bald, shining head there are only about fifteen hairs, which he brushes carefully into place every morning. This is his only relaxation. For the rest of the day he attends to really serious matters. He is Minister of Gravity. It is he who repealed the old King's Fireworks Law. All fireworks and festivities are now forbidden. People must work hard and take life seriously, and no nonsense!

One morning, seventeen years after the King's death, Minister Sure is sitting in his study in the Palace. The sun is shining into his room, so he has closed the shutters. Someone knocks on the door.

"Come in!" he calls out.

In comes his colleague, Mr Strait, Minister of Honesty.

"Am I disturbing you?" Minister Strait asks diffidently.

"Not at all. Take a chair, Strait. What can I do for you?"

"This morning," says the Minister of Honesty, "I discovered that old Gervaas, our butler, has worked for fifty years in the Palace—thirty-three years for the King and seventeen for us."

"Is that so!" exclaims Sure.

"It seems to me only right that we should throw a little party for him."

Minister Sure jumps at the word "party".

"Parties are dangerous, Strait; you know my feeling on the matter. They keep people from doing their duty. Think of something else, please."

"A ribbon?"

"Yes, that's more like it, I think."

They decide that Gervaas will be given the Order of the Bison, fourth class. Minister Sure pushes a button and the old servant appears.

"What can I do for you, Excellency?" asks Gervaas.

"Nothing. We want to do something for you, Gervaas. Minister Strait tells me that you have served in the Palace for fifty years now. Had you thought of that yourself?"

"Yes, Excellency," says Gervaas, very shyly.

"We have decided to make you a member of the Order of the Bison, fourth class. What do you say to that?"

"I know what you can do with your Order," Gervaas thinks to himself, but aloud he says, "I don't know what to say, sir, it's too much!"

"Oh no, you have certainly earned it," says Minister Strait cheerfully.

"Is there anything else we can do for you?" asks Sure.

"Yes, sir," replies Gervaas, much to the astonishment of both Ministers. "I would very much like you to receive my nephew, Stark."

"Your nephew Stark?"

"Stark was born seventeen years ago, on the awful night the King died. The next morning my brother, his father, fell off the tower, and his wife died of shock a few days later. Since that day I have looked after the child as well as I can."

"Well, well, well! You've never mentioned this before, Gervaas."

Gervaas is silent. Would the Ministers ever have listened?

"Why do you want us to receive your nephew?" the Ministers ask.

Gervaas fumbles awkwardly with his cap.

"It is he who wants it. He has something to ask you," he stammers.

"I greatly regret," says Minister Sure, "that I am too busy to receive boys of seventeen. What about you, Strait?"

Minister Strait does not relish the prospect either, but he cannot possibly tell a lie.

"Let him come to me tomorrow at ten. I'll talk to him."

"Thank you, Sir. Good morning, Your Excellencies." The newly-invested Gervaas leaves the room.

The following morning Stark sits facing Minister Strait. Minister of Honesty, just think of that! You can see from his face how difficult it is. His lower lip is raw because he bites it whenever problems arise. Quite often he shuts his eyes and wonders if he is really speaking the truth. For years he worried about beginning a letter with "Dear Sir" when he detested the person he was writing to. He has tried using "Detested Sir", but that has given great offence. Now he omits the opening words altogether. Nobody seems to notice. Even at home Strait has many difficulties. He is always catching out his wife and daughters in small lies. His two sons prefer to study abroad.

"So you are Gervaas's nephew," he begins

"Yes, Your Excellency," replies Stark, looking the Minister fearlessly in the eye.

"And you want to ask something?"

"Mr Strait, you Ministers have had seventeen years to find a new king. Nothing has happened yet. I have come to ask you what one must do to become King of Katoren."

The Minister of Honesty is dumbfounded. Never has anyone dared to ask such a question. He shuts his eyes and thinks very hard.

"If you had put this question to the Minister of Diligence your head would have been cut off immediately."

"Why?" asks Stark, quite taken aback.

"Because your question implies that you disapprove of our reign."

"Quite right, I do." says Stark.

"Shame on you!"

"I thought you would appreciate my honesty."

"Listen, my boy, I shall try to forget what you've said. Ask me something else, something innocuous, so that I can at least report some small thing to my colleagues."

"Minister Strait," says Stark, "I ask that you put the following question to the Council of Ministers: How can I become *King of Katoren*?"

"This will mean your death."

"Let me tell you something. I rang all the national newspapers, telling them what I was going to ask. There is now a crowd of

14

journalists at the Palace gate waiting eagerly to hear your answer. Don't you think it would look rather bad if your only reply was to parade my head on a stake?"

Minister Strait grits his teeth. He is surprised that the subservient butler should have such an upstart nephew. Not that for one moment does he regard this boy as a serious threat to the Ministers, but he is afraid of the journalists. They are always trying to catch one out in the smallest errors and make headlines of it.

"I'll put your question to the Ministers," he says stiffly. "I'll let you know in due course. Is that all?"

"Yes, sir, that is all."

"Good-day."

Stark goes away and gives a press conference. Minister Strait stays behind, quite flabbergasted. His lower lip is sorer than ever.

Weeks go by. Stark hears nothing from the Ministers. He learns from Uncle Gervaas that the Council is meeting regularly, but that the Ministers cannot come to any agreement. Neither Stark nor his uncle know that two of the Ministers favour banishing Stark, two others want him beheaded, while the remaining two want to give him seven difficult tasks to carry out.

"That is what happens in the old stories," says Minister Strait. "It will satisfy the people's sense of justice."

"Moreover," asserts Minister Kleen, "it's a simple enough matter to find seven tasks that are so difficult to accomplish that he will go home and cry on his uncle's shoulder before he has even finished the first."

Minister Rush thinks all this is much too complicated. He likes to get things over with. That is why he is Minister of Diligence. "No more talking, just chop off his head!" he cries, as he notes down his own words, and everything else that is said, in a little notebook.

Minister Watch agrees, but Ministers Sure and Good are for banishment. At long last, as they still cannot agree, they decide to cast lots. They ring for Gervaas.

"Gervaas, please bring dice," Minister Sure orders. Gervaas, who feel ssure that this concerns Stark, brings the dice in a leather cup.

"A one or a two will mean Off With His Head; a three or a four, Banishment; a five or a six, Tasks. Throw the die, Gervaas!" Trembling all over, the old man shakes the cup and places it on the table upside down. He does not have the courage to lift it. Minister Rush gets impatient, reaches out, and lifts it himself.

"Six. It's the seven tasks, then. Sure, it's up to you to set the first one. You should certainly be able to think up something difficult enough. Now I've got to go and give a lecture on the life of the ant. Good-bye." And he hurries off.

The other Ministers get up, too.

"Tell your nephew to come and see me at ten o'clock tomorrow morning," says Minister Sure to Gervaas.

The old man nods happily, and as quickly as his gouty legs will carry him, he rushes home to tell Stark.

That evening Stark asks his uncle for the two-hundredth time to tell him about his dream, and also about the night the King died. Is he really predestined to become King of Katoren? He goes up to his little attic room to look through his few poor treasures: a portrait of his mother, his father's trowel, a bundle of the old King's writings, given to him by Uncle Gervaas.

He takes the trowel in his hand and thinks, "If I can't be King, I'll be a bricklayer like my father. It's a fine trade." But deep in his heart he is convinced that he will become King. He is seventeen, just the age when you know you can slay every dragon, giant, or witch. Stark reads some of the King's writings, mostly proverbs. He can't fathom their meaning, but he likes them all the same.

Next morning's interview is very brief. Minister Sure sat up most of the night trying to decide upon Stark's first task, and now he feels sleepy.

"Take that smile off your face, young man!" he says sharply. "Life isn't as happy as you think it is. You won't laugh when you hear what you have to do."

"Please hurry up and tell me, then," says Stark.

"It seems to me that you'd better abandon this whole crazy plan. You're playing a very dangerous game. I don't know yet

16

what will happen if you fail, but if you take my advice, my dear boy, you'll put these fine ideas out of your head and become a butler, just like your uncle."

"Thank you very much," says Stark.

Minister Sure is a stern man, who has worsted many an enemy in his time, but he feels a kind of pity for the boy sitting in front of him with such a fearless look in his eyes. So he says hopefully, "You mean you'll abandon your task?"

"No," says Stark, "I mean that I thank you for your advice. I shall not follow it, because not all advice is good advice."

"You are dangerously bold, young man. Who taught you that?"

"My uncle," says Stark.

Minister Sure raises his left eyebrow. "Well, the decision is yours. Your first task is to put an end to the cries of the birds of Decibel."

"Marvellous, Your Excellency! I'll put an end to the cries of the birds of Decibel!"

"So you don't think that is very difficult, then?"

"Not particularly, sir," says Stark, who has never even heard of the birds of Decibel. "Very kind of you to make the first task so easy."

"Don't rejoice too soon. Here is a contribution from the government towards your expenses." He hands Stark an envelope.

"Thanks a lot, Minister."

"All the best to you."

Stark leaves the Palace and gives the news to all the waiting journalists. At home he opens the envelope. It contains a second-class train ticket to Decibel. One-way only.

He buys a week-end bag, a few shirts, a piece of string, a pocket-knife, and some other useful odds and ends. He reads in all the newspapers about his task, and how impossible it will be for a boy of seventeen to succeed where so many learned people have failed. Then he takes leave of his Uncle Gervaas, who, now that the time has come, is sorry he has landed his nephew in such a risky situation. The train leaves Wiss. Stark is looking forward to the future. Off to Decibel! The first step on his way to becoming King!

2

The Birds of Decibel

Decibel lies in the north-east of Katoren, on the edge of the foggy ocean, with a few rocky, inaccessible islands looming offshore.

Stark has never been away from Wiss before. It is the only town he knows. Standing in the centre of Decibel he feels very lost and lonely. The people all hurry silently along strange-looking streets with strange names, taking no notice of him. They don't even talk to each other. And they are all wearing very odd hats. Stark wonders about this. Stark has decided that he will pay a call on the Mayor before he does anything else. The Mayor should be able to tell him what the trouble is with the birds. He goes up to a passer-by.

"Excuse me, could you tell me . . .?"

The man walks on as if he hasn't heard.

"Madam, could you tell me . . .?"

"Ladies, could you tell me . . .?"

No response from anyone. Don't these people understand him? He gives up and walks on down the street. Perhaps it will lead to the town hall. He is beginning to feel very homesick, when suddenly a front door is pulled open and a woman rushes towards him. She has an apron on, as if she is preparing a meal, but she, too, is wearing one of these curious caps that cover the ears.

"Come in, come in!" she shouts, pulling his arm urgently. Stark follows her, too astonished to protest. What does the woman want? Once he is safely inside she slams the door.

"Shame on you! How could you do it?" she scolds.

"What have I done?" asks Stark, surprised.

"Come in here."

In the room a little boy of four or five is playing with his building blocks. He does not look up as they come in.

"Hallo," says Stark. The boy does not respond.

"Hallo," he shouts. Still the child takes no notice.

"It's no use, he wouldn't hear you if you brought an army of trumpeters."

"Is he deaf?"

"Once he got out when I wasn't looking and ran into the garden without his ear-protectors on," says the woman bitterly. "And that was the moment they came. For the first time in a week!"

"Who did? The birds?" Stark begins to get an idea of the problem.

"Who else? Where've you been all your life? Ah, that explains it! You're a foreigner. Now I understand why you were out without your ear-caps. I was so frightened when I saw you. If the birds had come just now you would have become as deaf as my poor boy Harco here."

Stark asks her to tell him what happens when the birds come.

"It's happened as long as people can remember, sometimes as often as every two hours, sometimes not for weeks on end. The trouble is, all the birds shriek at exactly the same high pitch. The sound they make is so shrill it could burst your eardrums! And that's why everyone always wears ear-protectors outdoors. Even inside the houses the noise is so disturbing that most people keep their ear-caps on all the time."

Stark tells her that he has come to Decibel to silence the birds.

"You silly boy," says the lady, "how can you possibly hope to succeed where so many brilliant professors have failed? Most of them have gone deaf in the attempt, and now they spend their time inventing new, improved hearing-aids. We're the world leaders in the hearing-aid industry, you know."

"Hmm, yes, I can see you have a problem here," says Stark pensively. "Now I'd better pay my respects to your Mayor."

The friendly woman explains how to get to the town hall, and gives him a spare pair of ear protectors.

"They're my husband's, but please keep them. He has at least ten more sets in his cupboard."

"Fine! And thanks very much." Stark pats little Harco on the head and goes out on to the street.

He hasn't gone very far when a terrible piercing shriek blasts through the air. He claps on the ear-protectors, but feels as if the sound is cutting right through his whole body. The air is full of thousands of black birds. The people in the street don't take any notice at all; they seem to be used to it. Stark shudders, thinking about what would have happened to him if Harco's mother hadn't been around. He sits down on a bench until the birds have all disappeared. Then he sets off again for the town hall.

The Mayor of Decibel is the most talkative man Stark has ever met. He invites Stark to his house, and talks without stopping all the way home—with his hands, his body, his plump cheeks, his head—with every part of him. "Now take Alderman Moven, for instance," he argues. "He claims he can put down the birds. He has a theory, which I won't explain to you now. He's been working on it for years, but the birds are still there. What do you think you can do, my dear boy, that he hasn't already thought of?"

"We'll see," says Stark.

"You see, you don't even live here. Alderman Whit also has his pet theory, which he brings up at every Council meeting. Now there's a really able man! He knows nearly everything there is to know about birds. If a specialist like Alderman Whit can fail, you . . ."

"We'll see," repeats Stark.

". . . You will certainly not be able to do anything. I have a little hypothesis of my own, if I can just think of a way to make it work. I'll explain it to you some time. I don't want to discourage you, but as a man of some experience I really must warn you that you have no chance at all."

"We'll see," is all Stark says.

He has taken off his ear-protectors in order to hear what the Mayor is saying. He sees that his host still has his on, and realizes that the good man has not heard a word. He walks up to him, lifts one of the protectors, and yells into the Mayor's ear, "We will hear!!" The Mayor gets the shock of his life, then he laughs heartily.

"You're right," he says. "It is difficult to hear anybody with these things on. On the other hand, you don't miss much!"

"I should like to know more about these theories of Alderman Moven and Whit, and also about your own," says Stark.

"Hey! You really listened to me?" The Mayor seems quite

20

surprised. "Tell you what, come with me to the Council meeting tonight. They're sure to expound their plans, and I'll tell you mine, too."

"Thank you, sir, I'll be glad to come."

The Mayor's wife is kind and hospitable, and no less amply-built than her husband. She serves up a delicious meal and invites Stark to stay with them—even though he gets such a fright when the birds fly over again that he spills a spoonful of red-currant sauce on the new carpet.

In the Council chamber Stark sits in the public gallery, watching all the councillors coming in, laden with piles of documents. The Mayor hammers on the table, opens the meeting and invites Alderman Moven to speak. He speaks for an entire hour, but what he says, in a nutshell, is this:

"If the birds torment us, we should torment them. If they make a sound that is unbearable to us, we must make a sound that is unbearable to them. To find a sound that will do the trick."

Mr Moven has captured a few birds and put them in a cage in his garden. When he hits the dustpan with a brush they squawk loudly, but often it is on a different pitch from that of the free birds. Mr Moven hopes to find out which sound the birds dislike most. He then proposes that all the people of Decibel will make this sound together, and thus chase away the birds.

Stark is astonished to discover that it has taken Alderman Moven a whole hour to explain this simple plan. However, it seems quite a reasonable idea. It might even work, Stark thinks. He himself is the only person listening. All the councillors are reading the papers, busy writing, or just dozing.

Then a gentleman suggests erecting a glass dome over the whole town, and a lady councillor favours evacuating everybody to another district. Neither of these ideas appeals to Stark.

He takes more notice of Alderman Whit. His idea is to capture a flock of the birds and to teach them different sounds, then let them go free, in the hope that the rest of the birds will copy them. Like Alderman Moven he keeps a few birds in a cage in his garden. The trouble is that they are so frightfully conceited. They never imitate your whistling: if you go high, they go higher. If you whistle low, they whistle lower still. The Alderman thumps the table and repeats himself over and over, but finally, to Stark's relief, his long speech comes to an end.

Last of all it is the Mayor's turn, and because he knows that someone is actually listening to him he speaks with real enthusiasm. He has developed a poison that will weaken the bird's vocal cords and thus stop the terrible shrieking. The only problem is to find a way of making them eat the poison. They very seldom settle on the ground, so poisoned grain would be no use. Perhaps shooting poisoned peas into the air . . .?

Stark is tired of listening, but he has a few ideas, now, and it does not seem as though it would be too difficult to silence the birds. He has a plan, which he will work on tomorrow. For the present, all he wants is to get some sleep. He is dead tired.

"Well, how did you enjoy the meeting?" asks the Mayor, when they are back in the house.

"Very interesting indeed. The solution seems quite clear."

But the Mayor does not hear.

Next morning Stark wakes up completely refreshed. He has slept very well. Wonderful beds they have in Decibel! He has something very important to do today, he remembers. What . . .? Ah yes, the birds. He knows how to silence them.

But does he really know? Yesterday when he was tired and not thinking very clearly, it had all seemed so simple. Now, in the clear light of day, he doesn't feel so sure of himself. He thinks of five hundred reasons why his plan might fail.

He gets up, takes a bath, and dresses. Then he murmurs to himself, "If all these councillors and the Mayor are thinking even a little way along the right lines, my plan *must* work!" The Mayor's wife has made him a good breakfast. She looks fresh and wide awake. With her husband still safely in bed, she talks a great deal. Stark hardly listens—he is busy working out his plan—but it doesn't matter, his hostess is quite content if he says yes and no occasionally.

After breakfast he strolls into town in search of a radio shop. Presently he comes across the firm of J. Holder & Sons. Mr Holder himself is at the counter.

"What can I do for you, my boy?" he asks.

"Sir, I see you sell electronic equipment."

"What is it you're looking for?"

"I was wondering if I could get an instrument that can control pitch and volume with just one knob?"

"Certainly you can. That is a sound-generator with a speaker attached."

"Fine! Then I want a sound-generator that can produce a very high pitch and a very loud volume."

"High, that's no problem at all. We can make a pitch so high that the human ear can't hear it. Volume, well, that will be more difficult. We shall have to put in an amplifier."

"Good. I want it to be more than a hundred times louder than anything you have ever sold before."

"Good heavens, then you'll need a houseful of amplifiers! That will cost one thousand pounds at least."

"I only have one pound fifty," says Stark.

"That's nothing like enough!"

Stark leans over the counter and whispers, "How would you like to see in the papers 'The birds of Decibel are silent, thanks to the equipment of J. Holder & Sons'?"

The shopkeeper shrugs his shoulders. "These birds cannot be silenced, not even with the wonderful equipment of Holder & Sons."

Then Stark explains his plan, but Mr Holder will not change his mind. Stark is just leaving to try someone else, when the Sons of Holder & Sons walk in. As soon as they hear the word "Birds" they want to know exactly what the problem is, and take off their ear-protectors to hear. They like Stark's plan and think they should at least give it a try.

"Come on, Dad, let's take a chance. If it doesn't work we'll get our equipment back."

"Covered with bird droppings, I suppose," says Dad.

"We'll clean it off," say the sons eagerly.

"I've heard that one before. I'll be the one who will have to do the cleaning. Well, go ahead then, boys, you can try. Get what you need from the store."

A few hours later the steps of the town hall are covered with dozens of loudspeakers and amplifiers. The sons connect them all to the sound-generator in the Mayor's dining-room. They put their names prominently on all the different pieces of equipment and go home. Fortunately the weather is fine, so nothing gets wet.

Stark sits by the generator, waiting. Nothing happens that day, or that night, or the day after. On the third morning the weather forecast is "scattered showers." Mr Holder comes and tells Stark that he doesn't want to risk his valuable equipment in any bad weather. Just as he says the words "bad weather", it happens. Thousands of birds fly screaming over the town.

Stark turns the knob. It takes a few moments for the generator to warm up, then a sound as loud and as high as the birds make shrills out from the loudspeakers. Stark turns the dial. His pitch is now higher than the birds'. For one moment they are silent. They seem astonished. Then they start again and, oh wonder, they scream on a higher pitch too! Eyes sparkling, Stark turns the knob again. The birds try to scream still higher. Again Stark twists the knob. The plan is working perfectly: the higher the birds scream, the higher the pitch from the loudspeakers.

"Now here goes," mutters Stark, and twists the knob round as far as it will go. A terrible squawking is heard as the birds try to cry still higher, then pang . . . pang . . .pang! pang! pang! pang! The vocal cords of the tormentors of Decibel can be heard snapping, one after the other. A minute later, not one bird can make a single sound.

Stark switches off the generator. An uncanny stillness falls over Decibel.

The people all think they have gone deaf. They can still *see* the birds, and seeing them without hearing them is inconceivable. Then they hear themselves coughing, they hear doors banging, and footsteps, and gradually they realize that they are not deaf at all. Those who live near the town hall see the young stranger coming out of the Mayor's house, looking up at the sky, then taking off his cap and ear-protectors. They see the Mayor rushing out of the town hall, snatching off his ear-caps, and throwing them on the ground and treading on them. He embraces the boy and dances round the square with him.

Then everyone rushes out of their houses. They all take off their caps and throw them in a big heap. They start talking to each other; they shake hands as if they were meeting for the first time. They try to sing—but who has ever sung in Decibel?

"We'll learn, all right," says the Mayor. He has climbed on to the statue of Gatsonius the Deaf, the inventor of the first ear appliance. "We'll soon be the best singers in the country. Thanks to Stark, this marvellous boy, the miracle has happened. Come and stand next to me and tell us how you did it."

"I just listened to the plans of Aldermen Moven and Whit, and to your own: a bit of one, a bit of another, and it couldn't fail. However it happened, the vocal cords have been snapped."

"But the young birds, what about them? Won't they do the same as their parents?"

"I hope not," replies Stark. Now that their parents cannot teach them that single pitch, I think they will sing at different pitches, as birds normally do; but if ever they start again, you know what to do about it."

There is feasting in Decibel for seven days and seven nights. Everyone gets very drunk, especially the Mayor. An old man has kept a fire-rocket in a corner in his attic, from the days of the old King, before the Ministers had made fireworks illegal all over Katoren. He sets it off, and the whole population cheers at the shower of falling stars.

"The old King once wrote, 'It is better to see one rocket in the sky than ten in the cupboard'," says Stark.

"Let's keep this little celebration a secret," whispers the Mayor, who is not quite drunk enough to forget that Minister Sure will be furious if he ever hears of the rocket.

Stark gets the Medal of Honour of the town of Decibel, and is also invited to choose a gift. The only gift he wants is a train ticket home to Wiss. The Mayor thinks this is much too small a present, but by this time his tongue is too thick to argue about it, so he invites Stark to come back to his town some time to receive a more impressive reward. Then the people of Decibel see Stark off at the station. They throw confetti over him and rub his hair with cognac. The girls all kiss him and want to marry him, but Stark only waves his arms. Then the train starts to move and soon he can see nothing more of Decibel than a swarm of dots in the distance.

25

3

Powdermill

Back in Wiss, Stark embraces his uncle, pats his little dog, Quick, and puts on a clean shirt. Uncle Gervaas is bursting with pride. The papers are full of Stark's success, and he can't get over his nephew's new fame.

"You are destined to become King of Katoren, I know it!" he says over and over again.

"Let's wait for the next task," suggests Stark. "Perhaps I will have to jump from the tower of St Aloysius, and that would be the end of that."

There are rumbles of discontent in the Council chamber. The Ministers are not entirely pleased that Stark has succeeded, and so quickly at that. It looks as if their plans have misfired. Minister Rush, the Minister of Diligence, is particularly put out. He tries to pretend that he is not impressed by saying, "What a shame I had no time to go to Decibel. I could easily have dealt with the matter myself."

Mr Rush is a hard worker, one must grant him that. He runs around from early morning until late at night. He pokes his pointed nose into everything. He writes as many as ten reports a day. He even writes with both hands at once—really, it's hard to believe. He can dress in two minutes and seven seconds, eat his breakfast walking down stairs, and kiss his wife while putting on his hat. He cannot imagine anyone wanting to relax. His staff go through life with a hunted look in their eyes and die from heart attacks at an early age.

"You, Kleen," he says to the Minister of Hygiene, "you were all for this task business. You think up the next one, and please make it more complicated than the first. Otherwise we'll soon have a seventeen year-old king who doesn't even know how to write a report, and who is sure to be as lazy as the rest of this bone-idle country."

A week later Stark is sitting opposite the Minister of Hygiene. They don't take to each other at all. Minister Kleen has a shining face and the cleanest hands in Katoren. He washes his feet three times a day and puts on a clean shirt every four hours. At home, his wife and children go about with handkerchiefs in front of their mouths, so as not to breathe in germs. The Ministry of Hygiene looks just like a hospital. All the officials walk around in white overalls and carry clean cloths to wipe the door handles before they touch them. There are posters on the wall, saying things like, "I am a Soap Fan. I wash my hands before and after every meal."

Compared to the Minister, Stark looks very dirty. His nails are not very clean, and he still has a bit of bird-dropping from Decibel on his shoe. Minister Kleen spots it immediately and turns pale.

"Young man," he says, "I am on the point of fainting."

Stark gets up, full of concern.

"Shall I get you a glass of water, sir?"

"Please go away and get rid of that disgusting mess on your shoe."

Stark goes out and takes most of it off with a match. When he returns, the Minister, still rather pale, whispers weakly, "Aren't you ashamed of yourself?"

"If you say so," says Stark the Bold. "In Decibel this awful stuff was knee-deep in the streets."

No, there is really no chance of these two becoming bosom friends. Abruptly the Minister says, "You want a second task, I suppose."

"Yes indeed, sir."

"Do you realize that we will punish you if you fail?"

"No sir, I realize nothing of the sort," replies Stark firmly.

"Silencing the birds of Decibel was rather an easy task, but the people will now expect something more from you. If you fail you will disappoint them sorely, and that is no light matter to responsible Ministers."

"Really?" says Stark.

"Here is your train ticket to Powdermill. Your task is to cut down the pomegrenade tree."

"Well in that case, I think I'd better go and buy an axe."

"I think a suit of armour would be more appropriate," says the Minister. "Good morning."

Outside the Palace the journalists are waiting. Stark tells them about the second task, and they rush off to set the presses rolling. Unlike the last time, Uncle Gervaas is optimistic.

"It seems an impossible task, but I'm convinced you'll make it."

Next morning Stark is in a train again. Powdermill is on the south-west border of the country, and the journey will take thirty-six hours. The station before Powdermill, a girls gets into his compartment. He thinks she looks smashing. She is about sixteen, with straight, brown, shoulder-length hair, and wears jeans and a multi-coloured jacket. Like Stark, she looks as if she isn't afraid of anything.

"Hi," she says offhandedly.

"Hello." Free and easy as they are, they don't quite know how to begin.

"Are you going to Powdermill?" he asks at last.

"It's the only other stop."

"Oh yes, of course it is."

"My name is Kim."

"Mine is Stark."

"Stark? You're not *the* Stark, of the birds of Decibel, the one who's coming to cut down our pomegrenade-tree?"

"The very person."

"Are you really?" I can tell you something, you'll never do it."

"Why not?"

"Man, the whole world has tried. Every officer with more than three pips has written a book about it. My father has two book-cases full of them. There's even a monthly magazine devoted to the problem called *NAT—News About the Tree*."

"Is that so?"

"Tell you what, Stark, I'll take you home with me."

"And put me in a glass cage, eh?"

"No, stupid, my father is Mayor of Powdermill, and he's expecting you. My mother likes having guests, and I don't mind them either."

"Fine," says Stark. "Now give me some NAT."

"News about the Tree—what do you want to know?"

"Everything."

"Well, to begin with, it's hundreds of years old. At first sight it looks just like a normal pomegranate tree—you know, the kind that has pinkish-red fruit with ever so many pips."

"Never seen one in my life. I guess my own town's too cold for them."

"Well, for the past fifty years or so, the Tree's been sprouting pinkish-red hand grenades instead of pomegranates. When they fall to the ground they explode. The trouble is, the Tree blossoms and bears fruit the whole year round, so we can't get at a fruit to cut it open and examine it. Two years ago Colonel Lion, the commander of the bomb-disposal unit, tried it in a tank, with a dip-net fixed to the end of his gun-barrel. We all heard the most tremendous explosion, and the Colonel flew into the air, tank and all. All we found was the top of his little finger."

"Surely you found a little bit more than that!"

"Well, yes, perhaps a little bit more. He got a military funeral, and I had to put a wreath on his grave, being the Mayor's daughter, you know."

"If these grenades are powerful enough to destroy a tank, why haven't they blown up the tree itself?"

"Oh, they do a fair amount of damage—but the Tree is so enormous that it doesn't matter, and the blown-up bits heal very fast. You have to understand—the tree trunk is so thick you could build a road through it."

"Why don't they just put fifty cannons round the Tree and shoot it to pieces?"

"They've tried that too, but what with the cannon-blast and grenades exploding, all the windows in the town were blown out, and walls began to crack and things like that. So they had to stop at once."

"And you just leave it at that?"

"What else can we do? We stay miles away from the Tree, and all our windows have been quintuple-glazed with extra-strong panes. It's a nuisance, but there it is."

"Jolly nice girl," Stark thinks, his spirits rising. "What a piece of luck to meet the Mayor's daughter on the train."

29

"How are you going to tackle our problem tree?" asks Kim curiously.

"No idea."

"Will it take long, do you think?"

Stark shrugs his shoulders. "Maybe I won't be able to do it at all."

At Powdermill Kim and Stark get off the train and walk into the town. It doesn't seem to be a very big place. Stark notices that all the cars are parked under little sheds in the street. He asks Kim about them.

"When there's an explosion, tiles and things fall off the roofs, and people are scared of damaging the nice, smooth paintwork on their cars." Kim snorts disdainfully.

They cross a big square and walk down the main street to the town hall and the Mayor's house.

"Look, there's the big church," Kim points out, "where they buried the remains of the Colonel."

"Beautiful windows," remarks Stark.

"A present from the factory, some years ago, when they had their fortieth anniversary."

"Factory?"

"Yes, outside the town. Nearly everyone in Powdermill works there. My father has a lot to do with it, too."

At the Mayor's house, Kim's mother is just going out.

"Mother, this is Stark," says Kim. I met up with him on the train."

"Well, Stark," her mother greets him, "welcome to Powdermill."

She takes his hand in both of hers. "It's good to see you here. Of course, you can't hope to do anything about our Tree—the Tree will last for ever: but it's good to be reminded of that again. I'm awfully sorry, I have to go out now, but I'll see you later. Kim dear, show him to the spare room. There's cold meat in the fridge, and plenty of bread left."

"Where are you going?"

"To the S.T. I must hurry, or I'll be late for the gurgle song Bye, bye!"

"Bet you can't guess what the S.T. is," says Kim, going towards the kitchen.

"Saving Teenagers?"

"No!"

"Serving Tea?"

"Wrong again."

"Sewing T-shirts?"

"You're miles away. No, it's the Society of the Tree. They're a group of ladies who think the Tree influences our lives, just like the stars, or something."

"I get it, Scorpio, Libra, and so on."

"That's it. They're crazy. They sing hymns, and sometimes they gurgle to it with pomegranate juice. That's their gurgle song. They make skirts of leaves, and everything they use in their rituals has to be made of wood. You know the sort of nonsense."

"I must have a look, some time."

"You can't. Men and boys are never admitted. I expect they'd make fun of it all."

While they are talking Kim prepares a meal, and Stark realizes how hungry he is. Just as they finish the Mayor comes out of his study to greet Stark. He seems to be extremely energetic, darting round the room with an armful of books. He is very friendly, but not the type of man to sit talking in an easy chair for very long.

"Stay as long as you want," he says hospitably. "I'll tell you everything you want to know about the Tree, but you'll find most of it in the books in my study. Mind you, it'll take you a few years to read them all."

"I don't intend to," replies Stark. "I would rather follow the teaching of our dear departed King: 'One rocket in the air spreads more light than a hundred cases of fireworks in the loft'."

Next morning Kim and Stark go to "Treeview", a restaurant whose main attraction is an excellent view of the Tree. Looking through the telescope provided for guests (at a small charge), Stark gets a splendid view of the phenomenon.

"Seems just like an ordinary tree to me," he says, but his words have scarcely passed his lips when a tremendous explosion makes him jump out of his skin. Kim doesn't turn a hair.

"If you turn the telescope a little you'll see the powder mill," she points out.

"What a bang that was! Was that a pomegrenade?"

"What do you mean, a bang? Oh that! Yes, that was one of them."

"You said 'powder mill'?"

"That's right."

"Do they make gunpowder?"

"Gunpowder, rockets, all sorts of munitions."

"Then the explosions come from the factory, I expect."

"Oh no, it's not as simple as that. The explosions come from the Tree, that's the one thing we're quite certain about."

"So it's just a coincidence that the powder mill is so close by?"

"Other people have had the same idea, but no one can find a connection between the mill and the Tree."

Back home, Stark goes straight up to the Mayor's study.

"What can I do for you?" asks the Mayor. "Do you want to know more about the Tree?"

"I want to know", Stark says, "how an ordinary apple grows."

"But Stark, my boy, didn't you learn that at school?"

"I only went to school for a very short time, just long enough to learn to read and write. Apart from that I know nothing."

"Ah, I see. Well then, it begins with the blossom, that's to say, the flowers. Each flower has a receptacle, in which you will see the pistil and the stamens. If a little pollen from the stamens gets embedded in the pistil, an ovary is formed, from which the fruit grows."

"So that's how it works. But how does the pollen get to the pistil?"

"Well, some of it may stick to an insect—a bumble-bee, for instance, and the bee will carry the pollen to the pistil; but it could also be carried by the wind."

"Your Honour, that factory near the Tree is a powder mill, isn't it?"

"Yes, indeed."

"And that high chimney, does it carry grains of gunpowder in its smoke?"

"Of course. What are you trying to get at?"

"I'm wondering if perhaps the gunpowder lands on the Tree's pistils, so instead of producing fruit, the flowers produce grenades."

32

"I've often wondered about that myself, but it seems pretty far-fetched to me. And even if that is the answer, how can we do anything about it? You can't avoid a certain amount of fall-out from a big factory like that."

"I beg your pardon, sir, but that does seem to me a *very* likely explanation—in which case your problem is solved."

"But how?"

"Just close down the factory."

"Impossible!" cries the Mayor, waving his arms in despair. "The whole population earns their living in that factory. The town would be ruined."

Stark scratches his head.

"Tell me, what happens to all the stuff you produce?"

"It is taken to the central munitions depots, where it is stored."

"What do they do with it all?"

"It's there in case we have a war with Eltory—you know, the country on our northern border."

"It's thirty years since we had a war with Eltory. Surely we've enough stuff stored up by now?"

"Well, you see, our spies tell us that the Eltorians build more and more munitions depots every year, because we do. We can't afford to fall behind. Surely you understand that?"

"All I understand is that it's a crazy way of living."

"Agreed, but no one can figure out how to change things."

"Sir, if the manager of the powder mill were to have the powder-sacks filled with brown sand and peat-dust, and sent them to the central munitions depots, what would happen?"

"Well, I think the Ministers ... the generals ... the admirals ... the officials ... well I think, really, nothing at all would happen. Nobody would notice."

"Tell him to do it!"

"But they would find out sooner or later."

"And then?"

"They would probably empty the sacks into our parks, and hang me."

"Why you?"

"Because I am the Chairman of the Board."

"The what?"

33

"I'm the boss."

Stark leaves the room, lost in thought, narrowly escaping a lyrical exposition by Kim's mother on the subject of the Society of the Tree. He wanders through the town, eating chips from the fish-and-chips stalls, jumping every time a grenade explodes on the Tree. The sun and Kim's hair are both shining brightly, and the birds are singing at the top of their voices. But the chimneys of the powder mill are belching black smoke—busy filling more arsenals with the tools of destruction.

"And to think that *people* say that *geese* are silly," he mutters to himself.

After a few days Stark gets used to the violent explosions that disturb the peace of Powdermill. He spends most of his time wandering through the town, deep in thought, on his own or with Kim. The Mayor's wife tells him that he can stay as long as he likes. He hardly ever sees the Mayor, but sometimes Kim kisses him when they sit together in the park.

One day, he wanders absent-mindedly out of the town, without noticing where he is heading. He is racking his brains, trying to figure out how to stop the local munitions industry without ruining the town's economy. Beware, Stark! Mind where you're going! You're walking too close to the Tree! You're past the red Danger line!

"Hmm . . . sacks of peat-dust . . . ship them to the arsenals . . . maybe a year before someone would notice. But what about Kim's father? He'd be the one they'd blame. That's no good. Someone else would have to—but that's no good either. They'd hang whoever it was."

BANG! The blast knocks Stark off his feet.

"Have I been hit? What happened?" He sees blood on his hands. He struggles to his feet and staggers painfully back towards the town. He feels so giddy that he can hardly walk, and just manages to get across the red Danger line before he collapses.

Two park-keepers find him half an hour later. They improvise a stretcher by putting two rakes through the sleeves of an overcoat, and carry Stark to the Mayor's house. They know who he is, of course, because he's become quite a familiar figure.

Kim is frantic when she sees her friend carried home on a stretcher, but she keeps a cool head and rings for a doctor. The doctor examines Stark's injuries, dresses the wounds, and gives him a blood-transfusion. The Mayor brings him round with a little cognac.

"He'll be all right," the doctor assures them, "but you must keep him in bed for several weeks."

"That's no problem," Kim says firmly. "Just so long as he gets well. I'll take care of him."

She sits by his bed all night long, gives him sips of water, fluffs up his pillows—in short, she behaves like anyone whose hero has been wounded. For days on end Stark lies in a semi-conscious state, delirious, half-way between dream and reality. "Mr Smith," he mutters over and over again. "We must have Mr Smith." Kim wonders who this Mr Smith can be.

It is the Mayor who finds out. One morning as he sits by Stark's bed, the boy looks up and says, "Mayor, you should appoint Mr Smith Chairman of the Board."

"Who is Mr Smith?"

"He doesn't exist. Write to the Council of Ministers, saying that you are too busy with your duties as Mayor and that you are appointing Mr Smith to take your place. Later, when they discover the sacks contain peat-dust, say that Mr Smith has fled to Eltory. Everybody will think he was really a spy."

The Mayor sits up straight, a gleam of interest in his eye.

"And what do the workers do in the meantime?"

"Let them make fireworks. But don't put the gunpowder in them yet. Keep them for later on . . . for when I am King. Then you can sell them to all the people of Katoren."

Is Stark delirious again? It sounds like it.

" 'Blue stars, red and yellow stars are better than stars and stripes', says the King," he mutters.

The Mayor leaves the room, deep in thought. Stark's accident has upset him very badly. His mind made up, he sits down at his desk, takes a pen and a piece of paper, and writes the following letter:

35

Your Excellencies,
Because of the overwhelming pressure of town council
work, I have appointed Mr J. P. Smith in my place as
Chairman of the Board of the gunpowder mill. I know Mr
Smith to be a very able and responsible person. His ex-
perience in the . . . etc. etc.

Slowly Stark recovers from his injuries. Kim goes back to school.
The Mayor's wife is busy with the S.T. Stark lies in bed reading
book after book from his host's library. The powder mill has
stopped producing gunpowder. On the orders of the invisible Mr
Smith, who prefers to give his instructions by letter, the mill has
begun to manufacture fireworks. All the workers are in on the
secret and have promised not to tell anyone. It's business as usual
at the powder mill; but the workers fill the sacks marked *gunpowder* with a harmless mixture of brown sand and peat-dust and
send them to the national arsenals. Meanwhile the warehouses at
the powder mill itself are filling up steadily with all sorts of
fireworks.

Stark keeps a log of the number of explosions per day. For
the first few days he sees no difference.

"Oh, but that's to be expected," explains the Mayor when he
comes to visit Stark (which he does every evening). "It takes at
least two months for the fruit to ripen."

Sure enough, two months pass and Stark's daily count shows
that the number of explosions are actually decreasing. People
begin to notice. There are headlines in all the papers. But no one
can quite figure out the connection between the reduction in explosions and the boy who wants to be King. What can he do from
his sick-bed in the Mayor's house? Rumour has it that he's more
than a little interested in Kim, the Mayor's daughter. But what
does that have to do with the miraculous change in the Tree?

Exactly four months and three days after Stark's accident, on
the very first day he is allowed out of the house, the last grenade
explodes. The people approach the Tree very, very carefully.
Keeping a safe distance they examine the fruit through telescopes,
to make sure that only ordinary pomegranates—and no explosive
pomegrenades—are left.

36

The long nightmare is over! A party of local officials brings axes and saws and cuts down the Tree. But old fears die hard, and many citizens make a prudent retreat into their cellars while the Tree is felled. The more passionate members of the Society of the Tree tear their hair, beseeching their neighbours to leave the Tree alone or beware the wrath of Heaven. But no one listens to them. The Tree falls. The officials chop it into small pieces, and throw every last splinter into a great bonfire.

Meanwhile, back at the Mayor's house, Stark quietly packs his suitcase. No one must ever know the true story of how Stark solved the problem of the Tree, or the Mayor of Powdermill would be in grave danger for his part in the plot.

"Until you're King, of course," the Mayor says to Stark. "And then I'll tell the world!"

The Mayor sits down and writes two letters to the Council of Ministers in the capital city of Wiss. In the first, which he sends by post, he informs them that Mr Smith, previously Chairman of the Board at the powder mill, has resigned without giving notice. The Mayor advises the Ministers that he himself will return to fill the vacancy.

"I'm afraid we'll have to start manufacturing gunpowder again," he sighs. "But only temporarily . . ."

"As soon as I am King I'll put a stop to it," Stark consoles him.

The second letter is for Stark to hand personally to the Ministers.

Meantime the square is full of people calling for Stark. "I can't let them see me. They'll ask all sorts of sticky questions that I can't answer."

"We'll go out by the back door. I'll take you round the back streets to the station," the Mayor promises.

"No, I will take him," says Kim decisively.

Are those tears in her eyes? They certainly are glistening. Leaning out of the carriage window Stark kisses them dry.

"Perhaps you'll be a Queen one day," he comforts her.

"When you need me I'll come!" she calls after the disappearing train.

Stark blinks, and for a long time all he can see are her two eyes shining as bright as the stars.

4

The Third Task

Uncle Gervaas and Stark have exchanged a few letters during Stark's illness, so Gervaas is expecting his nephew. From his small savings he has bought a bunch of flowers—the kind he knows the boy likes.

"Home again," says Stark. "What beautiful flowers!"

"You have a scar behind your ear." Uncle Gervaas has seen it straight away. "We didn't count on that, did we? Where's the girl?"

"At home, of course."

"I thought you would bring her with you."

"Oh no, she has to go to school. How are the Ministers?"

"They've heard that you cut down the pomegrenade tree, but they don't seem very pleased about it. How did you do it?"

"That is a secret."

Uncle Gervaas looks disappointed.

"A secret even from me?"

"Well . . . I suppose not. I'll tell *you*. It's like this . . ."

"So if there is a war with Eltory, our soldiers will load their cannons with peat-powder?" Uncle Gervaas is a bit worried. "The soldiers of Eltory won't run from that!"

"If the earth explodes, we'll all be sitting on the moon," retorts Stark. During his convalescence he has been reading books on space-travel.

He revels in being back home. He enjoys sleeping in his own bed, rummaging among his own things, and playing with his own dog, Quick, who is mad with joy at seeing him again.

Gervaas asks the Ministers when they can receive Stark. He comes home crestfallen.

"They say you did not carry out your task. You were ill in bed and the tree died by itself."

"Just what I expected. I don't think they like me very much," says Stark. "But I have a letter from the Mayor. Will you hand it to Mr Strait tomorrow, Uncle Gervaas? He cannot very well suppress it, or the whole Department of Honesty would totter on its foundations." He hands the letter written by Kim's father to Gervaas.

"It shall be done, Your Highness."

Next morning, after Gervaas has seen Minister Strait, the Council of Ministers is called together and the letter read aloud. It says:

Your Excellencies,
I herewith express my gratitude to you for sending Stark to our town. He has overcome the plague of the Pomegrenade Tree. How he did it I cannot reveal to you, because his life would be in danger, but it was he, and he alone, who achieved the miracle. In performing this heroic task he had to get so close to the tree that he was gravely injured. I hold this young man of Katoren in great esteem. His courage is beyond praise.
I am,
Your obedient servant,
The Mayor of Powdermill.

An impressive seal proves the authenticity of the letter, and if Kim's father does not always stick closely to the truth, Minister Strait is none the wiser.

Suddenly the Ministers begin to take Stark seriously. The boy seems to have ability, he is achieving as much as they hoped . . . or as they feared? It's all very fine to see some of Katoren's problems being solved, but it rankles that the papers praise Stark and criticize them.

"We must take care the boy does not become too conceited," volunteers Minister Good. "It could ruin his character."

Mr Good is Minister of Virtue. He rarely attends Council meetings. Most of the time he is travelling round delivering lectures.

The others agree heartily.

"I am exceedingly glad that Decibel and Powdermill are

relieved of their troubles," says Minister Sure, "but that does not mean that . . ."

"We really cannot sacrifice this boy," Minister Good points out. "He could be spoiled for ever."

"I think three tasks will be enough," intervenes Mr Rush. He is afraid there is going to be a long discussion. "It is time we were thinking of more important matters. Who has a suggestion?"

"I have."

It is Mr Watch's voice. He is Minister of Order and Regularity. Five faces look towards him expectantly.

"The Dragon of Smog."

The Ministers nod approvingly.

"You cannot really ask that of him," protests Minister Strait, although he has nearly decided to support the idea. "It is only a few years ago that the Dragon of Smog swallowed an entire infantry regiment for breakfast."

"That was Colonel Power's regiment, wasn't it?"

"It was indeed."

"Ahh, so that's why I haven't seen the Colonel around the Club lately," remarks Minister Rush. He is the only Minister who ever goes to a club. He likes to be seen everywhere.

"Yes, he was swallowed, poor chap. Quite by accident. But they've erected a statue in his memory," says Minister Strait.

"Statues, bah! Too many statues in this country already, if you ask me," says Minister Kleen grimly. "And filthy pigeon-droppings on every one of them."

"Let's come to the point, gentlemen," pleads Mr Sure. "Do we decide on the Dragon of Smog, or do we look for something else?"

No one raises any more objections.

"Will you look after the affair, Watch? It was your idea in the first place."

Minister Watch takes on the job in spite of the havoc it will wreak on his carefully-organized time-table. For the Minister of Order and Regularity is a firm believer in the well-planned life, with nothing left to chance. He believes that regular habits and a precise routine promote good health and improve efficiency, diligence, dedication, honesty, sincerity, and a number of other virtues. There are, however, a few evil-minded gossips who say that there is something highly irregular about his passion for regularity. The Minister's hobby is forecasting the weather. He has one burning ambition: to discover a way to make rain fall only according to a pre-arranged timetable.

The following day Mr Watch summons Stark and tells him to go slay the Dragon of Smog. Stark is delighted. He's always wanted to meet a real live dragon. Uncle Gervaas is not so delighted. He remembers only too well the grisly headlines about Colonel Power and his ill-fated regiment.

"They say the dragon has seven heads," he tells Stark.

"That's nothing unusual for dragons," replies Stark nonchalantly. "They say you're supposed to cut off six heads, but leave the seventh alone. If you cut that one off the whole lot grow back again."

"If a whole regiment couldn't cut off those six heads, what makes you think you can?"

"It's the sort of job that's probably easier on my own, Uncle Gervaas. And I'm not bringing along a regiment: I'm travelling light, with nothing but my pocket-knife, a bit of string, and a clean shirt."

His little dog barks.

"So you want to come with me, Quick? Don't you know that dragons eat small dogs for breakfast? Besides, I need you to stay here and look after old Uncle Gervaas for me. I'm off then, Uncle."

"Good-bye, Stark. God bless you!"

In fine form after his short holiday, and badly in need of a haircut, Stark sets forth to conquer the Dragon of Smog.

5

The Dragon of Smog

Smog lies low in the interior marshlands of Katoren. It is a land of twisted alders and weeping willows. Pallid rushes stand motionless in marshy pools; and prickling brambles, stinging nettles, and wolfs-foot leave little room for more cheerful flowers. Poisonous snakes slip silently through the undergrowth, snatching at water-rats. Over this land of terror hangs a pall of dense, dark clouds. The dragon-fly seems to be the only creature of light in this place of death and destruction.

This is the home of the Dragon. Here he feeds on a diet of dead birds and rotten plants. Wherever he has dragged his tail, nothing will grow for a year. Whatever he breathes on withers. Whosoever looks into one of his fourteen terrible eyes suffers a horrible skin disease.

When Stark gets off the train at Smog, he immediately covers his nose with his handkerchief. The combined smell of sulphur, rotting vegetation, and old dragon-droppings is unbearable. Clouds of black soot drift slowly past the church steeple. Everything is covered with a thin layer of black grit. Eyes half-closed and nose firmly covered, Stark walks into the town. He is the only pedestrian. Everyone seems to travel in the little cable cars he sees moving overhead at a terrific speed. Their glass windows are shut tight, and dense, black smoke comes from their little chimneys.

"Heavens above!" thinks Stark.

The heavens, in fact, are nowhere to be seen. Stark sees wide streets paved with fine stone, and many cathedrals, whose domes and steeples are obscured by the smoke. The houses are like palaces, richly decorated with multi-coloured mosaics and graceful arches in gold, bronze, and marble. But how small the windows are! he thinks. It must be dark inside, for all the lights are on even though it is only midday. Plants grow in window-boxes outside each house—but what plants! Liverwort, lichens, toadstools, horse-tails, and other equally gloomy vegetation.

"Some people do have odd tastes," thinks Stark. In spite of all the splendour he feels depressed. He even thinks of taking the next train home, but decides against it.

"Come on, let's go to the Mayor," he urges himself.

The town hall and the Mayor's house are easy to find. Situated in the big central square, they look like veritable castles. A man in an elaborate uniform answers the door. Stark thinks he is the Mayor.

"I am the Mayor's butler," the man answers.

"Whatever does the Mayor wear, if his butler has such a splendid costume?"

"This is not a costume, it is livery."

"Well, at any rate, can I talk to the Mayor?"

"No, you can not," says the butler. "First of all, the Mayor is not at home. Secondly, you don't have an appointment, and thirdly, you are not properly dressed. You must wear a black tie."

"I don't have a black tie," says Stark, "but as to the appointment, I hereby request to see the Mayor this evening."

"Not without a black tie."

Stark is not over-awed by the butler, in spite of the impressive outfit. "Well, old boy, you just tell the Mayor that I, Stark from Wiss, am coming to see him. I have come to kill that old Dragon of yours."

"Our . . . ?"

"Yes, that's right, your old Dragon."

The butler is flabbergasted, even more so when Stark stands on tiptoe and whispers in his ear, "Look at your shoes, sir, they are full of dirty soot." Then at the top of his voice, "Good-bye, sir. See you tonight."

He turns away and surveys the town. Fantastic architecture, but how can people live in all that stench and soot? He goes into a restaurant for a cup of coffee, but sees from the menu that it costs £1. Really! He settles for a mouthful of water in the park. Ugh! What a foul taste! Scooping up a little in his hand, he sees it is crawling with tiny red worms. He throws it away in disgust. He spends the rest of the day visiting cathedrals, but although he sees more beauty than he has ever seen before, he has never in his life felt so depressed.

"That Dragon must be killed as soon as possible," he thinks.

That evening he pulls the ivory ball that hangs on the bell of the Mayor's house. The butler opens the door, and although Stark is not wearing a black tie, he is invited into the hall, and a few moments later is ushered into the Mayor's study.

The Mayor is about fifty, and is dressed in an ordinary, well-cut suit—much to Stark's relief. His hair is cut short, the parting straight as a die. Gold-rimmed spectacles perch on his narrow nose. Altogether he looks rather severe, and Stark is pleasantly surprised at the warmth of his greeting. He has read about Stark's visit in the papers. Like the Mayors of Decibel and Powdermill, he is convinced that Stark will fail.

"Even Colonel Power", he begins, "with . . ."

"With his regiment," Stark finishes. "I know, I know, Mayor."

"Poor boy, what can I do for you? Are you booked into a hotel?"

Stark shakes his head.

"Then I'll give you a room at the Hotel Dragonteeth. It is just opposite, on the other side of the square. It's the best hotel in town."

"How much will it cost, sir?"

"Not all that much, about £17 a night."

"Then I'll only be able to stay there for ten minutes, on my money."

"Oh, did you forget to bring any with you?"

"Forget? I don't have any!"

The Mayor is surprised. "How is that? Even my butler has half a million. Everyone in this town is a millionaire."

It is Stark's turn to be surprised.

"No matter," says the Mayor cheerfully. "You have come to do the town a good turn, so I think the town should pay your expenses." He lifts the phone and rings the hotel. He orders a suite, tells them to look after Stark in every way, and instructs them to send the bill to the town hall.

"Well, that's organized. Now, tell me how you plan to tackle the Dragon."

44

"Can you tell me something about the creature, sir?"

So the Mayor tells him how the Dragon pollutes the atmosphere with the fumes he breathes out; how plants and animals cannot live where he has passed; and how the Dragon vomits into the water, polluting it just like the air.

"I think it's not only the Dragon who's polluting the air," remarks Stark, refusing the cigar that is offered to him.

The Mayor smokes all the time. Stark has noticed people in the street smoking the same cigars. They smell foul.

"You're right about that," admits the Mayor. "We all smoke these strong cigars, so as not to smell the dragon-breath, you understand?"

"No," says Stark.

"What do you mean, no?"

"No, I *don't* understand. Why kill a smell by a worse smell?"

"You don't know the Dragon," sighs the Mayor. "You don't know what it means to have the smell of rotten eggs in your nose all day long."

"What about those cable cars above the streets? Very ingenious, but they produce an awful lot of bad air. Is that really necessary?"

"It makes them go faster, so we don't have to be out on the street for too long," answers the Mayor.

"Why don't you want to be out for long?"

"Because of the bad air."

"I must say, you live in a queer kind of town," says Stark, "I never saw such a rich, beautiful place, but nobody looks at it. How is it that your town is so rich, sir?"

"It's because everyone works all the time."

"Why do they always have to work?"

"Because they have nothing else to do."

"What?" exclaims Stark, surprised. "I have lots of nice things to do with my leisure time."

"What, for instance?"

"Well, I go swimming, I walk in the woods, or I just lie in the . . . sun," he concludes lamely.

"Just so. I see you understand me now. Well, young man, I've two reports to finish before tomorrow, so you must excuse me

45

now. Go away and have a good sleep in the Hotel Dragonteeth, and think up a workable plan to rid us of the Dragon. Oh, one thing: cutting off the Dragon's heads is useless—they grow again immediately. Colonel Power could have told you that, if he had not been swallowed. Good-bye."

The Mayor is once again the severe, elderly gentleman. He shakes hands formally and rings for the butler to show Stark out.

"You certainly do have long working hours," observes Stark to the butler.

"Only sixteen hours a day."

"Only!"

"Well, one doesn't really need more than eight hours' sleep."

"But surely you need a bit of time to yourself?"

"We don't like spare time, here in Smog. We prefer working. Good evening."

Stark's answer is heard only by his handkerchief, which he presses to his nose as soon as he is outside.

The Hotel Dragonteeth is very grand. Two porters rush up to Stark, and are quite disappointed when they see he has only a small weekend case. They carry it between them, each holding one handle. The rule of the Hotel is that a minimum of two porters must show a guest to his room. With really important guests the number may rise as high as ten! In the suite, his feet sink up to the ankles in the deep-pile carpets, the bed is large enough to sleep the whole Council of Ministers, and the bath is like a swimming-pool. Sitting amid all the golden candelabra, luxurious chairs, damask curtains, and costly pictures, Stark feels utterly miserable. Perhaps he misses Kim. He is beginning to hate this Dragon with a fervent hatred, and promises himself that he will kill it as soon as he possibly can. Then he sinks into bed and sleeps for ten hours.

Next morning, after a sumptuous breakfast on a silver tray, he drenches his coat and handkerchief with lavender water, takes his courage in both hands, and plunges once more into that stinking town. He wants to talk to people, but it's not easy—nobody wants to stay in the street a moment longer than they have to. At length he gets into conversation with a dustman.

"You see that dirty-yellow cloud there?" The dustman points. "Look, you can just spot it through the fog, there towards the south. That's probably where the Dragon is."

"Why is the cloud yellow?"

"Sulphur. He breathes out yellow sulphur all day long, or so they say. I've never seen him myself, thanks be, because if he looks at you, you're sure to get a rash."

"Does he ever come into the town?" asks Stark.

"Hardly ever. He seems to prefer the marshes."

"How did he come to swallow Colonel Power, do you know?"

"Oh yes, everyone knows the story. That morning the regiment left from the market-place armed with rifles and cannons. We all saw them off. The girls kissed all the soldiers, and the Mayor's wife kissed Colonel Power. It was the last kiss for every one of them, except Brass and Vorger. Those two soldiers returned the same evening, completely broken-up. They're both in a mental home now. What happened was this—they fired their rifles and let all hell loose at the Dragon—we could hear that for ourselves in the town. They destroyed one head after the other, but one head grew back as fast as another blew off. Meanwhile, the Dragon closed in and covered them all in yellow sulphur, then ate every soldier he could catch. The two survivors don't remember how they escaped, but Brass does remember seeing Colonel Power eaten. No, nobody can meddle with that Dragon," the dustman finishes his tale.

"Revolting!" says Stark, shuddering.

"Oh, you get used to it," replies the dustman. "The worst thing is the smell; nobody can bear that. People die young because of it. That's why dustmen are so well-paid, they have to spend so much time out in the open. I am the best-paid person in the whole of Smog." He looks at his gold watch, and turns to his job of emptying dustbins.

Stark continues his walk. He looks at the fungi in the window-boxes. He sees that the parks are full of toads and centipedes. Grey rats with long, bare tails swim in the ponds and moats. "Revolting!" he repeats. He goes back to the hotel and orders lunch.

"What would you like to drink, sir?" asks the waiter, who looks more like a general with a hundred medal ribbons.

"Water," replies Stark, reacting strongly against all this grandeur.

"You did say water, sir?" The waiter seems upset.

"Water," repeats Stark.

He looks on while the problem is discussed with a colleague. Then the waiter disappears into the kitchen and comes back with a jug of water, a sieve, and a spirit-stove. He sieves the water and shows the little red worms to Stark. He then adds a purifying pill to the water and sets it in a pan on the stove.

"You will understand, sir, that I can only serve you hot water," he apologizes.

"Why not keep a jug of purified water ready for use?" suggests Stark.

"It is seven years since we have been asked for a glass of water, sir."

"That I can well understand," says Stark, eyeing the worms. He eats with little appetite and spends the rest of the day strolling in the town. By nightfall he is decidedly the worse for wear, feeling lonely and depressed. It is ridiculous for the future King of Katoren to spend the whole day thinking about a girl of sixteen, but, much to his annoyance, he can't get Kim out of his mind. So he writes her a long letter.

"I think of you often," he writes. "It is so dreary here that my thoughts turn to the fine, sunny skies of Powdermill. By the way, will you please ask your father to send me two hundredweight of saltpetre and a couple of sacks of charcoal? The powder mill will have them in stock, and your father said I could ask for anything I needed." The letter ends with a few sentences for Kim's eyes alone, so we won't repeat them.

He takes the letter to the post-box and goes to bed. For the first time he understands how people can cry for hours on end over the sorrows of the world. He feels very much like that himself, but drops off into a healthy sleep instead. And that is the end of that day!

The next day, the citizens of Smog invite Stark to give a lecture on the sun in the town hall. Although Stark has never even been to a lecture, much less given one himself, he decides to have a go.

48

The whole audience glitters with diamond tiaras and gleams with gold tie-pins. The Chairman calls the meeting to order with an ivory gavel.

"We are very proud," he begins, "to have as our honoured guest tonight this very illustrious young man. Stark will talk about a heavenly body that most of us have never seen, but which has achieved considerable fame. Stark has been brought up in its light, and I'm sure we are all very eager to know what he has to tell us about it. Perhaps," he adds, with a twinkle in his eye, "he will even condescend to give us some indication of his plans for destroying the Dragon." (Polite laughter.) "I shall now hand you over without further ado to our speaker for the evening, Stark."

"Do I start talking now?" asks Stark.

"That's the general idea."

As we know, Stark has never been shy. He stands on the rostrum, perfectly at ease, looking out at the pale faces in the hall.

"Ladies and gentlemen," says Stark, "I hope you'll forgive me saying so, but you all look like death warmed up."

The audience shuffles its feet uncomfortably.

"This pallor," continues Stark, "is from lack of sun. When people's skins are constantly exposed to sunlight they turn a healthier colour. The people who live outside Smog are nowhere as pale as you are, except on their backsides, which are generally covered by trousers. I've often wondered why people wear trousers, and lately I've come to believe that this is a symbol of our sympathy for the citizens of Smog. If *you* have to do without the sunlight all the time all over your bodies, then it's only neighbourly for us to deprive ourselves on at least one small, insignificant area!"

Everyone laughs. Stark begins to tell them about the sun. He feels inspired by his theme as he thinks about Smog with its yellow sky, black soot, and foul water, and sees the men in the audience puffing on their stinking cigars. He speaks lovingly about the flowers that unfold their innocent petals to the sun, about butterflies that flutter in a thousand colours from blossom to blossom, about buzzing bumble-bees, dancing gnats, the

49

intoxicating scent of roses, about people who stretch out on the beach and let the sand run through their fingers.

He tells them about the spring behind his Uncle Gervaas's house, splendid cold, clear, spring-water with a pure taste. He talks about forests of fir-trees with their sharp smell of resin and pine-needles. He takes his listeners into a beech-wood in the early morning. The penetrating sun transforms the dewdrops into pearls strung on spiders' webs and makes of the wood a giant jeweller's shop in which everything is free. He climbs the southern slope of a mountain and lets his listeners sunbathe on a projecting rock.

Are the good ladies sighing? Are the honourable gentlemen flexing their flabby muscles? Are the white faces flushed with longing? Do these industrious people feel a flicker of a yearning for leisure and lazy sunbathing? Stark finishes to the sound of thunderous applause. He sits down beside the chairman and, slightly embarrassed now, asks in a whisper, "Is that roughly what you meant by a lecture?"

The chairman nods, "And a very good one, too," he says.

Then the people in the audience ask questions. Everyone wants to know how he intends to kill the dragon. Stark tells them that he doesn't know yet.

"Well, that's no surprise," says one very fat man.

A woman sighs. "Oh, if we could only feel the warmth of that glorious sun you've talked about, just once! A bright blue sky . . . the scent of pines . . ."

"You wouldn't see much of it even if you had it," replies Stark. "You're all so busy working all the time."

"But if we had the sun perhaps we'd work less. Goodness knows we're rich enough as it is."

Again and again the discussion turns to the Dragon. The people of Smog hate it more than anything else in the world. Everyone has a different suggestion for Stark about how he should attack it. He nods amiably, but he isn't really listening. He's concentrating on something that has suddenly struck him.

"There is something you could do for me," he says. "I want dead birds. If you find a dead bird, please send it or deliver it to me at the Hotel Dragonteeth."

"Aha!" says a man. "Now I know. You want to starve the dragon out. You plan to take away his favourite food."

"Oh, no," answers Stark. "You certainly can't starve a dragon out. If he got very hungry and couldn't find any dead birds to eat, he'd probably pay a visit to the town. And we certainly don't want that! No. I've something else in mind, but I don't want to talk about it, since I'm not sure it's going to work. But remember, I don't want you to kill any birds on purpose. If you find birds that have died of natural causes, I'll be happy to have them.

"That will be easy," says another man bitterly. "Birds die by the thousands in this place. Only the ravens survive, and even they seem to be dying off lately."

"I think it's time to bring this meeting to a close," says the Chairman, rising. "We have spent more than two hours here, and although it has been most informative, I'm sure we all agree that time is money and we must get back to work." He thanks Stark and closes the meeting. Everyone rushes off in the cable cars, leaving clouds of black dust behind them.

Stark presses his handkerchief to his nose once more and walks back to the hotel. He wants desperately to help these people —how could any good king do otherwise?

Two days later several large sacks arrive by rail from Powdermill. They are addressed to Stark at the Hotel Dragonteeth. There are two letters with them. One is from Kim. She writes that she hasn't been able to eat a thing for worrying about Stark and dragons. She also writes a lot of nonsense which has nothing to do with this story. In spite of the fact that he thinks half of what she says is rubbish, Stark reads her letter fourteen times over before he opens the other one, which is from Kim's father, the Mayor of Powdermill. He sends Stark all good wishes for his new venture, and confirms that he has sent two hundredweight of saltpetre and two sacks of charcoal, as ordered. He concludes, "I know you can look after yourself perfectly well, but please remember this stuff can be dangerous."

"Thank goodness for that!" murmurs Stark. "If it weren't I wouldn't have asked for it."

He is just about to re-read Kim's letter for yet another time when there is a timid knock at the door. The Hotel Manager comes in.

"I'm very sorry to disturb you, sir, but can you tell me when all the dead birds are going to be removed?"

"Are you worried about the smell?"

"Oh no, nobody will notice that, but they don't look very nice, and besides . . ." he hesitates.

"Besides?" asks Stark.

"I'm afraid the Dragon will smell them and come here for his lunch."

"You're absolutely right. I'll try to get them out of the way as soon as possible."

"Thank you very, very much, sir." Stark is now so well-known in Smog that even the Manager of this very grand hotel bows low before him.

Stark is very busy for the rest of the day. He sits on a chair in the hotel courtyard, wearing rubber gloves. He slits open each bird with a knife, one by one. It's a nasty job, but it has to be done. He puts a spoonful of saltpetre and a bit of charcoal inside each bird, then stitches it up.

"It's a horrible job," he tells himself, "but don't forget what the old King used to say: 'Even the biggest rocket needs a match to get it started.'"

It's after dark by the time he finishes. Satisfied with his day's work, he takes a bath to wash off all the slime and gore. Then he goes to visit the Mayor, who receives him very graciously and asks politely about his progress.

"Everything's going splendidly, sir."

"I'm glad to hear it," says the Mayor. "Is there anything I can do to help?"

"Yes, there's one thing, sir. Tell me, does anyone ever venture out towards where the Dragon lives?"

"The Dragoons," answered the Mayor. "They are the officials who go out to the marshes whenever it is necessary to check the water level, or gather medicinal plants, or anything like that. A dangerous job, I can assure you. But well-paid. They earn more than I do, as a matter of fact. We issue special protective clothing to every Dragoon. It's supposed to protect him from Dragon-rash. That's a nasty skin condition you can get if the Dragon breathes on you. But it doesn't really matter—if the Dragon meets a Dragoon he usually gobbles him up on the spot."

"Well, I'll need their help," says Stark. "I've designed a trap. I'll need the Dragoons to scatter a lot of specially-prepared dead birds in a place where the Dragon will find them. Today, if they can manage it."

"Of course."

"Then tomorrow, could they go back and see if the Dragon has eaten them?"

"No problem at all."

"That's splendid, sir. I've got the birds all ready in the hotel courtyard. Your citizens helped me collect them."

"If you're thinking of poisoning the Dragon, Stark, don't waste your time. Poison is mother's milk to that creature."

"I'll tell you my plan *after* the Dragon has swallowed the birds. I'll come back the day after tomorrow. See you then."

Stark leaves the Mayor, feeling rather pleased with himself. The butler shows him out. Stark would dance in the streets—if the filthy air of Smog didn't make it so hard to breathe.

The birds have been taken away, and Stark is waiting for news. On the evening of the following day he learns that all the Dragoons are safely back in town. They report that the Dragon has swallowed nearly all the birds. Stark goes back to the Mayor.

"Now I need a rifle, and one of those bullets that bursts into flames when it hits the target."

"I'm afraid we don't have anything like that here," the Mayor tells him. "We are civilized people, and we use only civilized rifles. And we don't have many of those. Why do you need it?"

"Let me explain," says Stark. "This Dragon of yours is full of sulphur, breathing out yellow clouds and fumes and all. Right? Well I've learned a thing or two about sulphur during my visit to Powdermill. For instance, did you know that gunpowder is made of saltpetre, charcoal, and . . . sulphur?"

"Well?" The Mayor sounds interested.

"I've filled those dead birds with saltpetre and charcoal. If that mixes with the sulphur inside the Dragon, the Dragon will be . . ."

"Full of gunpowder!" shouts the Mayor

"If I'm right, the Dragon is probably a walking explosives-factory at this very moment. But what can we do about it? I thought that if you had one of these incendiary bullets I could try to fire a bullet straight into the Dragon's mouth. And if it caused even the tiniest spark, the Dragon would explode."

"What a brilliant idea!" exclaims the Mayor. "What a shame we don't have the proper bullet."

"Are you absolutely positive you don't, sir?"

"You'd have to go back to your friends in Powdermill for that sort of thing."

Stark and the Mayor are both silent, thinking hard. Suddenly Stark jumps up.

"Rockets!" he cries. "We could do it with rockets! Don't you have any fireworks here?"

The Mayor goes very red in the face. "How can you even ask such a thing? Don't you know that fireworks have been against the law for over seventeen years? In fact it will be eighteen years to the day tomorrow."

"That's right! Tomorrow's my eighteenth birthday! But tell me, are you sure you don't have one little firework hidden away in your attic somewhere? Put by for the next King's coronation, perhaps?"

"How dare you accuse me! . . . Well, to be quite honest, I think there might be one that I might have forgotten about. But no one must ever know!

"No questions asked," promises Stark, "but I must have it."

The mayor is panting by the time they reach the attic. "It's eighteen years since I've climbed these stairs," he puffs. He unlocks a long wooden chest and brings out a star-shell and a firing-gun.

"This is the only one," he said. "Don't forget, I could go to prison if word got out about this."

"Don't worry," Stark reassures him. "The secret is safe with me. But why did you keep this one?"

"As you guessed. To celebrate the next coronation. I used to love fireworks once—but that was in the old days, when the last King was alive . . . Now promise you won't tell a soul!"

"Not a soul ," repeats Stark.

"It's only one rocket, remember. If you miss the first time you're lost. He'll devour you on the spot. Maybe you'd better give up the whole thing."

"Oh no, I'll be all right!" Stark hides the fireworks under his coat as he crosses the square. In the privacy of his hotel room he examines them carefully. For the first time he feels nervous.

The rumour spreads through the town—Stark has gone off to the marshes to find the Dragon. Even the hard-working citizens of Smog look up from their labours every few minutes to peer anxiously at the yellow clouds in the distance. Everyone old enough to remember (and that's everyone over the age of five years) thinks of the late Colonel Power and his regiment.

At the town hall the officials are busy placing bets. The odds are twenty to one against Stark. Some Dragoons arrive, and everyone rushes up and tries to pump them for information. One Dragoon announces that Stark has borrowed his special dragoon-suit to protect himself from the dreaded Dragon rash.

"He's a nice boy," says the Dragoon. "It's a pity the Dragon will eat him . . . pity about my suit, too!"

Eleven o'clock . . . twelve o'clock. The yellow clouds still hover ominously in the distance.

Meanwhile, Stark slowly drags himself through the marsh, his large Dragoon-boots sinking up to the ankles in the boggy ground. It is easy to find the way: head for the yellow fog and you'll find the monster inside it. His heart starts pounding. Stark, carefree, unflappable, Stark, suddenly realizes what a dangerous mission this is. Has the mixture really turned to gunpowder inside the Dragon? Will Stark be able to hit the Dragon with his first and only shot? He's never even tested the firing-gun. Will the rocket work after eighteen years mouldering away in an attic?

Eighteen years. "Well, it's my birthday today, after all," he thinks, feeling better. "How could anything go wrong on my birthday?"

55

He looks at his watch. Twelve o'clock.

Wait! He hears something! A soft swishing sound. He can't move very well in the large boots, but he goes as fast as he can and hides behind a weeping willow. He clutches the gun so tightly that his knuckles turn white. The swishing gets louder, and he can hear a shuffling noise and a splash. Any second now the monster will emerge from the yellow cloud. Stark holds his gun at the ready. His nerves are strained to breaking point. Will he be dead five minutes from now? Or will Smog be free of the Dragon for ever?

"You're all right, Stark. Keep cool. You're all right," he says to himself over and over again.

The Dragon appears! It lumbers out of the yellow fog about a hundred yards away from Stark's hiding place. Its seven heads wobble on seven swaying necks. The forked tongue darts in and out of the evil mouth. Its body is covered in scales, and the enormous legs end in cruel, curved claws, like the talons of a gigantic bird of prey. The tail alone looks strong enough to kill twenty men at a single blow.

His knees trembling, Stark takes aim at the third head on the right—it seems less wobbly than the others. He murmurs a quick prayer and pulls the trigger. Within a split second he knows he's missed. The gun must have moved as he fired.

But the Dragon has seen him. Fourteen eyes look towards the willow tree and see the rocket coming. The monster never misses. The last head on the right swoops out and catches the rocket in mid-flight. There is a burst of flame, and Stark presses himself close against the tree. Then, with an earth-shaking roar, the Dragon explodes into ten thousand pieces.

The blast throws Stark to the ground. He's stunned for a minute, but when his head clears he ventures a look round. The top of the weeping willow lies broken off beside him. On the spot where the monster exploded he sees a large crater in the ground. It's beginning to fill up with marshy water. He notices a few fragments of dragon-flesh clinging to his boot. Suddenly he sits up and stares. Horrible! The bits of dragon are moving! Little dragon-heads begin to sprout, and tiny tails! An icy hand of horror clutches his throat. What has he done? Ten thousand dragons! Ten thousand hungry dragons eating up Smog, gobbling Katoren, devouring the world!

Stark shuts his eyes to block out the ghastly vision. He doesn't see what happens next. The explosion has stirred the air into a whirlwind, a tornado that sweeps the sulphur clouds away. The sky begins to clear, and for the first time in living memory the sun shines over the marshes of Smog.

Stark feels its unexpected warmth through his anti-Dragon suit. He opens his eyes and looks down at his boot. He opens them wider. Can this be possible? The tiny dragon is shrivelling into a small heap of brown dust. He begins to understand. It's the sunlight! The only thing that could kill the Dragon. No wonder the old beast surrounded himself with clouds of sulphur! All around him tiny dragons are turning into dust.

He stands up and turns his face to the sky. Never in all his life has he loved the sun so much!

The city of Smog has gone mad. When they hear the explosion in the marshes, everyone rushes out of their offices and workshops. They see the air clearing. They feel the warm sun on their pale faces. By the time Stark gets back to town the main square is full of people, cheering, shouting, singing in the streets. They've made an enormous scrap-heap of sooty cable cars, cigars, and anything else that fouls the air. They pour petrol over the lot, set it alight, and dance around the bonfire.

The Mayor spots Stark, and rushes over to him. But Stark can hardly recognize the Mayor. The honourable chief citizen of Smog has grime on his face, his tie hanging loose, and three buttons missing from his waistcoat. He nearly smothers Stark in a joyous embrace until the crowd hoists their young hero on to their shoulders and begins to parade him around the square.

"Name your reward. Whatever you want! Tell us your heart's desire and hang the expense! Jewels? Money? The key to the treasury?"

"I'd like a one-way ticket to Wiss, please."

"You must be joking! First of all, you must stay with us so we can show you our appreciation. Secondly, we'll make you a millionaire."

"No thank you," Stark replies. "First of all, your city won't stay rich for very much longer. Now that people have got a taste of basking in the sun, they won't be willing to work so hard. You'll have to face up to that. And, secondly . . ."

"Secondly, what?"

"Secondly, I didn't do it for money. A good king has to help his people because he loves them, not because of any hope of financial gain. As the old King used to say, 'A king who expects reward is like a volcano: high and mighty but not to be trusted.' So I ask you only for my train ticket home. There are still four more tasks I have to do."

The Mayor escorts Stark to the station, buys him a ticket, and waves him good-bye with the tattered remains of his mayoral waistcoat.

Stark leans back, exhausted, against the cushions of the first class compartment. He can see the smoke from the bonfires rising into the sky.

6

The Ministers Are Annoyed

Minister Sure enters the Palace with a bundle of newspapers under his arm. All his colleagues are present in the Council chamber, except for Minister Good, who is away in the country lecturing on The Fruits of Virtue. He throws the papers on the table.

"Just listen to this," he says.

Katoren Times: STARK CONQUERS THE DRAGON!

Wiss Messenger: STARK DOES IT AGAIN!

Katoren Herald: DRAGON OF SMOG SLAIN BY STARK!

Morning Sun: THIRD TASK FINISHED—DRAGON SLAIN!

The other Ministers leaf through their newspapers nervously.

"This boy certainly seems to be rather talented," says Minister Strait, after reading the article in his newspaper.

"No doubt," says Sure, "but his methods are really irresponsible. Imagine putting powder in a dragon! The animal could have been split in three; you never know how dragons will behave. Then there would have been three dragons at Smog. So, though I admire the boy, I hesitate to set him any more tasks. We had better put the whole thing off until he is thirty."

Most of his colleagues nod, but Watch shakes his head.

"Impossible, gentlemen," he says. "*They* would not stand for that." He points to the newspapers.

"You're right, of course," replies Sure.

"It's very annoying," says Minister Rush. "All these mayors who send us letters about their problems, and not one mentions how easy they are to solve. Look what we got this week: nearly a thousand letters, all begging us to send Stark to them."

"Have you read all these letters, Rush?" asks Minister Kleen.

"Of course!" The Minister of Diligence is offended.

"And did you find a suitable task for number four?"

"I did indeed. Up till now the boy has had to deal only with

59

living things—birds, trees, dragons. Let's try him on dead things for a change."

"What have you in mind?" asks Sure.

"Churches."

"Are churches dead things?"

"I mean buildings—big stone church buildings."

"What's the problem with them?"

"Come on, boys, you're not trying," snaps Rush.

Minister Watch laughs aloud.

"Of course, Ecumene!"

"Agreed?" Rush asks the others.

They nod. Rush rings the bell and Gervaas enters.

"Will you get your nephew here as quickly as possible?"

"He'll be with you in ten minutes, Your Excellency."

Nine minutes later Stark stands before the Ministers. His shoes are still yellow with sulphur. He has not had time to clean them. He has not been to the barber either. Perhaps because of these two things he seems a shade more impudent.

"Although your actions put the people of Smog in considerable danger, we are satisfied that you fulfilled your third task," says Sure. "You now have the right to the next one. Mr Rush will give you your assignment."

"The Shuffling Churches of Ecumene," announces the Minister of Diligence.

"What are they, and where is Ecumene?"

"Ecumene is a town in the north," says Minister Rush. "Where's your geography, boy? The Shuffling Churches are churches that shuffle, and it is your task to stop them. You'll get your train ticket in tomorrow's post. Good morning."

Grinning from ear to ear, Stark looks round the circle of stern, unsmiling Ministers.

"We've no use for laughter here, boy."

"Funny thing, shuffling churches. When I sit in church my uncle always says I shuffle my shoes. But perhaps that's not the kind of shuffling you have in mind."

"Oh, those shoes! I can see them yet," shivers Minister Kleen.

"I do clean them once a week," protests Stark, annoyed.

Minister Strait covers his face with his hands, and whispers,

"Never tell lies in my presence."

"Oh well, not every week, maybe. It does become a drag."

"For pity's sake!" cries Minister Watch.

"Get going now," says Minister Rush. "We have many important things to do."

"Are you sure?" asks Stark, still grinning. "Good-bye, then, Excellencies. I'll let you know as soon as I stop the churches shuffling."

He bows, just a little too low to be polite, and leaves the Ministers not knowing quite what to make of him.

By this time Stark can't move anywhere without a little army of journalists swarming round him. As he leaves the Palace they rush forward, bombarding him with questions.

"Did you get a new task? Were the Ministers nice to you? Do you think you can fulfil all the tasks? What has been your most difficult task so far? Do you earn anything from them? Are there any tasks you've refused?" And so on and so forth.

"Gentlemen," says Stark, "the honourable Ministers have set me the task of solving the problem of the Shuffling Churches of Ecumene. There is no reward. This is the most difficult task to date, because it is the only one I haven't solved yet. But I'll have to solve it, otherwise Uncle Gervaas's dream won't come true. The only task I would decline would be jumping off the tower of St Aloysius. Now I must run. Thank you very much for all the kind things you've written about me in the papers; but do write something nice about the Ministers, too, then perhaps they won't look so sour next time I see them. Be seeing you."

Stark goes home and finds a fat letter from Kim waiting for him. She has read the story of the Dragon in the papers, and tells him for a whole eight pages how proud she is of him.

Life with Uncle Gervaas is now becoming a little trying, for he, too, looks on Stark as the future King.

"Be sure and read this while I'm away, Uncle," says Stark, handing Gervaas a slim notebook. It is in the old King's handwriting and is entitled: *The Higher the Rocket the Faster the Fall.* Next morning Stark packs his few belongings and heads once again for the station.

7

The Shuffling Churches
of Ecumene

The Mayor of Ecumene is kneeling in prayer in his private chapel, but his mind keeps wandering. The editor of the local paper has informed him that the celebrated Stark is on his way.

"I must warn you, sir," announces the editor, "that if there is any threat to our church there will be serious repercussions. Do not underestimate the power of the press."

"But Mr Cutter," the Mayor protests, "you know very well that I am a staunch supporter of your congregation."

This is quite true. No one is a more zealous pillar of any number of churches than the pious mayor of Ecumene. No one attends their services as faithfully as he; no one is so scrupulous about giving each church its fair share of attention.

But the Mayor has a secret. He has written to the Ministers asking them to send Stark to help solve his problem. He never dared hope that anything would come of his request, but it appears that Stark is on his way.

The Mayor puts away his Reformed Church prayer-book, and takes up the one from the Constructed Church. But it makes no difference—he simply can't keep his mind on his prayers.

"I'm not deluding myself," he thinks. "I know very well that this Stark will only add to our troubles instead of ending them. But I'm at the end of my tether. So what's one crisis more or less?"

The Mayor's kindly face clouds with grief as he thinks of the latest tragedy to afflict his citizens. Only last week the Newly Restored Church ran down the widow Rosamund. Poor soul. He had attended her funeral. If only . . .

"If only this Stark comes up with something! They say he's worked miracles. Strangling seven-headed dragons with his bare hands . . . If only . . . !"

Shaking his head, the Mayor of Ecumene turns to his Ecumene Cathedral Catechism and tries very hard to concentrate on its teachings.

"Hmm," thinks Stark, as he gets out of the little local train that has carried him on the last leg of his journey. "This place looks more like a village than a proper town."

The square outside the station is lined with lime trees. The houses are far apart. He sees a coach with a real horse, and some long, winding country lanes. The one thing missing is a church steeple. He doesn't see a single one. He had expected a big town with dozens of churches.

"I suppose I'll start with a visit to the Mayor," thinks Stark, strolling into the little town at a leisurely pace. It's a good thing he hasn't brought much luggage.

It doesn't take him long to find the town centre, which is a large, grassy oval called the Green, with a round bandstand in the middle. He sees an elaborately-lettered sign outside one building: *Ecumene Town Hall*. Next door is a large, inviting-looking house with blue shutters that must be the Mayor's residence.

Stark rings the doorbell and is greeted by a plump, middle-aged woman in black. She takes him to the sitting-room where the Mayor and his wife and their six children are having tea.

"You must be Stark!" exclaims the Mayor. "We were just talking about you."

He introduces Stark to his family. Mrs Mayor pours out a cup of tea, and the youngest child tries to untie Stark's shoe-laces. It's a warm, friendly, easy-going family, and Stark feels at home straight away. Mrs Mayor invites him to stay, and Stark accepts without hesitation. They make him tell all about his adventures, and hang on every word about the Dragon and the pomegrenades and the horrible birds. He wonders why no one brings up the shuffling churches of Ecumene, but doesn't want to ask.

Suddenly the Mayor announces, "I've got to go to the B.B.C. Would you care to come along, Stark?"

"What's the B.B.C.?"

"The Big Bell Church. It has the most enormous and most up-to-date amplifiers of any church in town.

"I'd be happy to come," says Stark.

"You don't mind walking, do you?" asks the Mayor. "At the moment the Big Bell Church is about a mile away."

"I like to walk," says Stark. "But if you don't mind my asking sir, what do you mean when you say it's a mile away *at the moment*? Does that mean it could be somewhere else tomorrow?"

"It could well be. I gather the Ministers haven't briefed you very thoroughly about our problem. Let me explain."

As they walk along Stark begins to perceive that the kindly Mayor of Ecumene is a sorely troubled man. He learns that Ecumene, in spite of its rustic appearance, is the largest municipality in the country of Katoren. He also learns that Ecumene has twelve churches. And all of them behave in a very unorthodox way.

"In the Middle Ages," the Mayor tells him, "the people of Ecumene built twelve churches. Over the centuries each one has been struck by lightning or destroyed by fire, rebuilt, re-designed, restored—all the things that happen to old buildings over the centuries. But the strange thing is this: they've started moving.

"You mean they move from one place to another?"

"That's right. They don't move very fast, but once they start nothing can stand in their way. They crush flat anything in their path, like steam-rollers."

"Good heavens!" cries Stark.

"I hope you don't mind my saying this, but I'd rather you didn't use the word 'heavens'. Perhaps you could say 'Dear me!' instead? Of course, I don't mind myself, but some of our churches are very sensitive about things like that. And I've learned that it never does to step on anyone's toes here in Ecumene."

"I'll try," promises Stark, and repeats to himself, "Dear me, dear me, dear me."

"As I was saying," the Mayor continues, "it is rather a nuisance, the way these steam-rollers—I mean churches—move around. People live in constant fear. At any moment their homes may be crushed flat as a pancake."

"I can see your problem," says Stark.

"We've tried to sort things out by appointing Church Conductors."

"Church who?"

64

"Church Conductors. We've ascertained that it is possible to exercise at least a small amount of control over the churches' movements. We can do various things to change their direction—moving the pews, opening windows, and so forth—even though we can't stop them moving altogether. We've got Church-conducting down to a science, and we usually manage to keep them on the right tracks."

"Right tracks?"

"Yes, you'll notice that we've marked out paths for the churches to move along. Church-tracks. As a matter of fact we've just crossed over one."

"I wondered what it was."

"Unfortunately, the churches sometimes veer off their tracks, and there's nothing the Conductors can do about it. Only last Friday night the Newly Restored Church flattened the house of old Widow Rosamund. And we couldn't do anything to save her."

"Horrible! Does that happen often?"

"Things do get out of control from time to time. If one church becomes unmanageable, the others tend to follow suit. That's why last week's accident is so worrying."

"By this time they've reached the B.B.C., or Big Bell Church. It is a handsome edifice, with two domes and four bell-towers. Stark is admiring the architecture, when he suddenly realizes that something strange is happening.

"It's moving!" Slowly but surely the colossal building starts lumbering towards the town centre, like some enormous monster.

"The B.B.C.'s really been on the move lately," the Mayor tells him. "Let's go in and see what the Conductor is doing to control it."

When they go inside the Mayor informs the Conductor that the Council has decided that the Big Bell Church should be diverted onto the western track, instead of moving towards the centre of town.

"What makes the Council think it can interfere with the direction of our church?" retorts the Conductor.

"Rest assured," the Mayor reminds him patiently, "it is our

official policy to keep out of church affairs. But you understand that after last week's tragic incident we must take some decisive action to prevent catastrophe."

"Well, I suppose you're right," grumbles the Conductor. "By the by, we missed you at services last night. Not losing your faith, are you?"

"You know very well that I am scrupulously faithful to all the churches. But last night I had to attend the N.R.C. because of the late widow Rosamund."

"The N.R.C. is always on the wrong track," sneers the Conductor.

"The pot calling the kettle black," says the Mayor reproachfully. "What about the new school building? Have you forgotten so soon?"

The Conductor reddens. "Well," he mutters, "everybody makes mistakes."

"I suppose it couldn't be helped," says the Mayor. "Never mind. Let me introduce you to Stark. He's come to solve our problems."

"I hope you're not planning to demolish our churches," says the Conductor warily.

"Oh, never!" Stark reassures him. "I suppose my job is to teach them how to stay on the straight and narrow."

"Another idealist!" snorts the Conductor. "The shuffling churches of Ecumene will never stop shuffling. And if the skill and training of Conductors can do nothing, what do you think a mere boy like you can accomplish? The shuffling churches will just go on shuffling."

"Do they shuffle backwards, too!" asks Stark.

"Indeed they do not!" retorts the Conductor indignantly. "Only forwards, always forwards!"

"Time we were going home, Stark," says the Mayor, shaking hands with the Conductor and wishing him and his church a safe journey.

When they leave the church they notice that is has shuffled several yards during their visit.

"It doesn't move very fast," observes Stark.

"Slowly but surely," says the Mayor. On the way home he tells

66

Stark about the controversies that have arisen over the churches' movements.

"The people of Ecumene are very proud of their respective churches. Each congregation wants its own church to travel along the nicest roads through the most attractive neighbourhoods, passing through the centre of town as frequently as possible."

The Mayor's wife has prepared a simple but well-cooked dinner, which is nearly cold by the time they start eating, because of all the prayers that have to be said to satisfy the creeds of twelve different churches. After the meal they play Blind Man's Buff with the six children, then Stark goes to his room, promising himself to spend some time thinking over the problem. Instead he falls sound asleep.

"Stark, wake up!"

He dreams the Mayor is pulling his arm. He opens his eyes—the dream is real.

"Get up at once, we have to leave the house immediately."

"Fire?"

"No, the N.C.R. I'll tell you later. Come on!"

Half-asleep, Stark pulls on his clothes. It is still dark outside. Downstairs a bustling crowd of people are carrying furniture out of the Mayor's house.

"What's the matter?"

"It's the N.C.R.—the New Church Rebuilt. During the night it got obstinate and shuffled right towards this house. It is not responding at all to the Conductors' efforts. If they can't stop it, our house and the town hall will be flattened within the hour."

Outside, the whole population is hard at work carrying things out of the town hall. Some twenty yards behind the Mayor's house, Stark sees an enormous church looming menacingly, its gothic spires still invisible in the darkness. Inside the church he watches the sweating Conductors carrying church benches from side to side, directed by the minister from his pulpit.

"How many yards left?" the minister cries to someone coming in.

"Eleven, the direction is still the same."

"Then take the organ. Throw it down!"

The men hesitate.

"I say, throw the organ down! It's the only thing left that may help."

With despairing looks, the men throw down the organ pipes. They land on the floor with a metallic crash.

"The south end, take them to the south end!" the minister calls out frantically, and to one of his assistants, "Go out and have a look at the direction."

The assistant is soon back. "No change," he says, discouraged.

Outside, Stark sees that there are now only two yards between the town hall and the church, and not more than four between the church and the Mayor's house. The Mayor's wife and their children stand huddled together on the Green looking anxiously towards the shuffling monster. Everything has now been carried out of their house. Stark goes towards them and the youngest child grips his hand. The Mayor comes up to his wife, all hope gone, saying, "It cannot be helped, my dear. Be brave."

All activity has ceased. The people stand watching on the Green, as if at the cinema. Daylight has come. One inch left . . . Now the church touches the town hall, and suddenly, as if a giant's hand had drawn a line, a large crack appears on the side wall. Is the roof moving? Yes, inch by inch it tilts forward. Now the whole building leans out, and with a mighty crash the town hall of Ecumene collapses. Many women weep.

"That's where they were married," the Mayor tells Stark, "and the births of all their children were registered there. In spite of all the quarrelling and fussing between churches, the town hall was the community house."

"We were married there too," sobs the Mayor's wife," and afterwards our marriage had to be celebrated in all twelve churches. It took a whole day. The people had prepared such a wonderful surprise for us. Do you remember, my dear? For weeks before they had been planning a perfect route, and on the wedding-day all the churches stood in a perfect circle, evenly-spaced round the Green. And now . . ." The poor woman sobs bitterly. The moving church crashes into the Mayor's house, demolishing it completely.

"All my six children were born there," says the Mayor in a low voice. "Each one was baptized in a different church, one of them in this awful church that has crushed our house. We wanted six more children, but now I am not so sure."

"Cheer up, sir." It is the Conductor of the B.B.C. they had talked to the day before. "We'll build you a fine new house."

Stark looks at the crowd. They all seem subdued. Nobody so much as shakes a fist at the church—not that it would make the slightest difference, but Stark feels a violent urge to do so. Gently he disengages the little girl's hand, puts it in her mother's, and walks away to try and think clearly. He must find some way to stop the churches moving, he simply must.

For days on end Stark wanders about the town of Ecumene. He has been given a little attic room in the house the Mayor has found for his family, but he is hardly ever there, except to sleep. He is out and about, talking to people, trying to find a new idea. All the churches keep to the church-tracks, moving in wide circles round the town centre. Ever since that horrible night, Stark has sensed something menacing about these moving giants. They are so merciless, so unyielding.

"They keep moving forward," muses Stark. "Nothing can stop them. I can't pull them down, and I can't get rid of them any other way. What in Heaven's name can I do?"

He examines each church carefully, inside and out. In the New Church Rebuilt he finds some people repairing the organ. The church is as quiet and gentle as a lamb now. Stark feels that the solution to the problem is right there in front of his nose, but he can't quite grasp it.

"Always moving forward," he mutters, "with nothing or no one to stop them. At the Mayor's wedding they made a circle round the Green." He concentrates so hard that his head aches. Then suddenly . . .

"Got it! What a fool not to have seen it! Plain as day . . . !" What a relief! He feels wonderful. With a burst of energy he rushes off to find the Mayor.

Can the Mayor arrange a meeting for Stark to speak to the Conductors?

"Nothing easier. As a matter of fact I have a meeting with all of them scheduled for tonight. It's our usual post-disaster session. We always call a meeting after an accident to try and analyse the situation. But so far nobody's been able to shed any light on the problem, and I don't expect we'll get anywhere tonight either—in spite of the fact that this last catastrophe was the worst on record. So we'll be very happy to hear your ideas, whatever they are. These will just be your first impressions, of course."

"Oh no, sir, I've got a plan."

The Mayor jumps out of his seat so fast that his Bible falls to the floor.

"A plan? A really workable plan?"

"Yes, I think so."

"You mean you have a way to stop the shuffling? Without demolishing the churches?"

"I think so, if everybody's willing to help."

"How? Tell me, tell me, quickly!"

"It's really very simple, sir." Stark explains his plan.

"It is so simple, my dear boy," agrees the Mayor, "that it has not occurred to anyone before. I'll back you up, if necessary, till I'm as hoarse as a cracked church bell." He walks away, shaking with excitement. Stark watches him go, and realizes he is very fond of the Mayor of Ecumene.

The Mayor takes the chair at the meeting that night. First on the agenda is a report on the disaster. He insists that no one was at fault, and that the Conductors clearly did everything in their power to prevent collision.

"My fellow citizens," he goes on, "in spite of all our efforts, we have never yet managed to prevent such catastrophes, but now I have news for you. You all know Stark: he has visited all your churches, and most of you have talked to him." The men nod.

"Well, Stark has a plan. In my opinion it is the plan of a genius, a plan worthy of a future King. Stark, be so good as to explain it to these gentlemen."

Stark gets up.

"It's quite simple," he says. "At the Mayor's wedding you arranged all the churches round the Green, I hear. So it seems possible to do that."

The men nod.

"Could you do the same thing again? They would all have to be there at exactly the same time. As they will all be coming from different directions, eventually they'll hit each other. Nothing can stop them, but they might stop each other. Then we would have one enormous church. Break through the side walls, and you'll have a building where all the citizens of Ecumene can meet together. There won't be another building like it in the whole of Katoren, perhaps not even in the whole world.

You could hear a pin drop. Then . . .

"Do you get it . . .? We simply make all the churches into one."

The uproar starts, everybody talks, argues, cries, cheers, criticizes, gesticulates, fights, slaps. Complete chaos.

The Mayor takes up a jug of water and dashes it to the floor with all his might. That does it. Everyone quiets down at once.

"I want no interruptions." This mild-mannered man thumps the table with such force that a chip of wood breaks off. "I am the head of this municipality and a member of all your churches. I tell you, I want this plan carried out just as Stark suggests. I will think it out tonight. Tomorrow morning you will all be given details of your route. Today week all your churches will meet at the Green at three o'clock precisely. The meeting is closed."

They all go home, and Stark sleeps a deep, dreamless sleep, but the Mayor sits up all night, working out an exact time-table. He marks the routes of the twelve churches in twelve different colours on the map.

During that long week of waiting, Stark does nothing but wander through the fields, write to his uncle and to Kim, and play with the Mayor's children. He calls twice at the Mayor's office, which looks more like the headquarters of a general at war. Large wall-maps show the position of every last house, every little lane. Small flags show the current positions of the churches. The Mayor neglects his religious duties entirely. Three telephones give him the latest information on church locations. If it happens that one church is behind schedule he marks out a shorter route, or a longer one if a church is moving too fast. He has bags under his eyes and hasn't shaved for days. Stark keeps offering to help, but the Mayor insists on doing everything himself.

"I'm responsible, so please don't interfere."

Everyone in town keeps their fingers crossed that no church will go out of control. In that case the whole plan would have to be scrapped, and a new one started from scratch.

"It'll be all right," says Stark. "I'm always lucky."

And so Thursday dawns—a Thursday that no one in Ecumene will ever forget. The Mayor has found his degree in physics a great help: he's figured out a perfect plan. By nine o'clock all twelve churches have arrived in a circle on the Green. While the others move round the perimeter, the enormous B.B.C. is shuffling towards the centre, where it will come to rest with the other churches grouped about it. The smaller churches will be placed behind it, to compensate for the strong push of the larger one. At twenty-five past nine the other eleven buildings begin to move inwards. Except for invalids and babies, the whole population of Ecumene is there to witness the miracle, in addition to journalists from all parts of Katoren. They try to interview Stark, but he retreats into the Mayor's office and closes the door.

An exhausted volunteer phones to say that one church is a yard behind schedule. Stark phones the Conductor, then turns to the Mayor.

"Everything's going splendidly. Leave the flags for a moment and come and watch it all happening. I do hope this is the last time the churches will shuffle, so come and take a final look." One of the phones rings. Stark lifts the receiver and says, "Please ring back in five minutes." He takes all the phones off their hooks and stands by the window with the Mayor.

Here they come, from all sides, their steeple roofs glittering in the sun. The flocks of crows round each spire begin to merge into one large flock. The route of the N.R.C. lies between two houses, with only a yard to spare on either side, but the colossus negotiates it safely. The Conductors are all in their churches, and all the volunteers are in their assigned positions, working flat out. Never have the people of Ecumene worked in greater harmony.

Tears well up in the Mayor's eyes and roll down his haggard face.

"The churches are uniting at last," he whispers. "I'll never forget this moment."

He wipes his eyes, then puts back the receivers. All three phones ring at once. He listens, makes notes, gives instructions, moves the little flags. Two o'clock: another hour to go. The B.B.C. is now very near the centre of the Green.

Stark, judging that the journalists will be too busy taking pictures to notice him, ventures outside to look round. It's now half-past two. The buildings shuffle on without stopping, closer and closer together. Now a pillar of the B.B.C. is touching the stick that marks the centre of the Green. The churches are now so close to each other that it is difficult to see exactly what is happening. A protruding angle of one church catches the window of another. That, the Mayor has not foreseen. One minute to three. A rasping sound of stone against stone is heard, and with a muted rumble the churches come to a halt. One turns through an eighth of a circle, to get closer up to the B.B.C. in the middle. A piece of mortar falls. On the Green there is a stunned silence. Here in Ecumene stands a building the like of which has never been seen before.

Slowly and solemnly the people approach, and enter through the many doors. Inner doors are lifted from their hinges, and inside windows knocked out. Only lack of tools prevents the people from pulling down the inside walls.

The ministers and Conductors come together and offer prayers from the many prayer-books. They decide on a hymn they all know. Soon, the mighty sound of twelve organs playing and thousands of people singing resounds through the building, and flows out through the numerous windows. It pours through cracks and bell-towers, winging its way to the pure blue sky.

Stark alone stays outside. He sees the door of the Mayor's office open. The Mayor steps out and comes slowly up to him. Standing together, the sound of the hymn all about them, the Mayor weeps with emotion.

Stark says, "Never mind, sir, no one is looking."

"You are right, my boy. See how they stand together in unity. Is it to this end that these churches have been shuffling all these years?"

73

Stark is silent.

"Perhaps it was necessary," continues the Mayor, "for the town hall to be destroyed. They could have gone on arguing endlessly and doing nothing. As it is, the disaster made such an impression on them that they agreed to the experiment."

"Possibly," answers Stark. "Now that I see the churches together I'm reminded of one of the old King's sayings. One of the few that don't refer to fireworks. He writes somewhere, 'Sometimes things have to get worse before they get better'."

"Come inside, my dear boy."

"I'm sorry, sir, but I have something else to do."

"Your fifth task?"

Stark nods.

"I'll see you off to the station."

Stark collects his few belongings and a little later climbs into the local train. The Mayor has bought a ticket for him.

"All the best to you, Stark."

"Thank you, sir."

"I'll come to your coronation."

The little train moves off. Stark hangs out of the window and waves to the Mayor. Long after he is out of sight, Stark can still see the church steeples of Ecumene, huddled peacefully together after so many years of separation.

8

The *Katoren Herald*

As soon as he gets back, Stark sends a written report on Ecumene to the Ministers. He also asks them to give him his next task. Uncle Gervaas delivers the letter by hand, so the Ministers can't make any excuses about it being lost in the post. You would think that Stark would enjoy a week's holiday at this point, but he's anxious to get all his tasks over with as quickly as possible.

Uncle Gervaas is getting nervous. He's watched the Ministers' faces get longer and grimmer each time Stark returns from another successful mission. He's afraid they're up to something. So he starts doing something he has never dreamed of doing in all his years at the Palace: he begins to eavesdrop. He crouches in a cupboard in the Council chamber for three hours, his ear to the keyhole. He comes home very depressed.

"They're planning to ask you to jump off the tower of St Aloysius," he tells his nephew. "They've heard that you said it's the one thing you'd never do. Minister Rush is the only one who's voted against it. Not because he's afraid you'll be killed—oh, no, nothing like that!—but because he's afraid of public opinion."

"Friendly chap, this Rush," Stark observes wryly.

"Minister Sure suggested they give you eight tasks instead of seven, but the Minister of Honesty wouldn't stand for it. 'Seven is seven,' he insisted. Then they stopped for lunch."

Stark begs Uncle Gervaas to promise him he'll never eavesdrop again—not because he shares Mr Strait's scruples about honesty, but because he's afraid of what the Ministers would do to his uncle if they found out. However, Uncle Gervaas ignores both his nephew's warning and the cramp in his legs, and resumes his post in the cupboard the very next day.

He comes home in a fury. "Those scheming so-and-so's!" he fumes, "You'll never believe what they've decided! They've

75

agreed to divide the fourth task into two parts. Task four (a) is the wretched tower. Strait and Rush finally agreed."

"Uncle Gervaas, you can't be serious! You don't mean to tell me they really expect me to jump off that tower. What a stupid waste!"

"They do indeed," says Gervaas, "and from the very place where your poor father fell to his death. But I won't hear of it. You're not made of rubber, you know. And don't get any fancy ideas about parachutes either. I forbid it. It's impossible."

"Impossible and pointless," Stark nods sadly.

Next morning he receives a letter from the Ministers, smothered in impressive stamps and seals. It says exactly what Gervaas already has told him: "Task Four (a): Jump off the highest gallery of St Aloysius Cathedral on Friday morning at ten o'clock sharp."

This time there is no eager sparkle in his eyes. He looks contemptuous and defiant.

"Uncle Gervaas."

"Yes, my boy?"

"I simply refuse to throw my life away doing something so foolhardy that doesn't help anybody."

"Of course you'll refuse. It's just plain suicide. I tell you what, I'll go up and ask them to give you something else."

"That won't help, and you know it. I'm going for a long walk in the woods to think things over. I'll be back on Friday morning at nine o'clock. Come on, Quick."

The dog jumps up and follows him. Uncle Gervaas stays behind. He takes up the letter, then leaves the house. He walks slowly to the office of the *Katoren Herald*, the most important paper in the country, and the only one strong enough to oppose the Ministers.

Kim dashes into her father's study. He has never seen her so furious. She throws down a newspaper angrily.

"Look, Dad, those beasts! How dare they?"

"Calm down, girl. What's the matter?"

"They want to make Stark jump off the St Aloysius tower."

The Mayor of Powdermill quickly reads the front page of the *Katoren Herald*. The headline says: STARK GETS TASK FOUR (A).

"Dad, I want to go to Wiss," says Kim. "Did you see the leader? The first sentence says, 'To blazes with Task Four (a)!' and asks everyone to come to Wiss on Friday. If only you'll give me money for the train, I can just get there in time."

The Mayor reads the article over again and nods.

"Of course, it's really meant for local people, not for country people like us, who would have to travel a day and a half to get there, but in our case . . . in your case . . . well, yours is a special case, Kim dear. It is rather a lot of money, but I'll get a return for you, yes."

"You're a darling." She kisses him on both cheeks. Her long hair almost sweeps the inkstand off the desk. "I'm off to pack my things."

As soon as Kim's mother hears about the journey she starts baking apple pies. Since the Tree troubles ended she has not had much to do. She bakes three—one for the journey, one for Stark, and one for his uncle. Meantime Kim has filled two large suitcases with all sorts of stuff. Her mother and father wonder what on earth she can be taking with her. They discover when they go to bed that night.

"It really is a bit much," grumbles the Mayor, but Kim's mother just goes into fits of laughter and gives him a pile of towels to rest his head on. "Kim's in love. What can you expect?"

By then Kim is hundreds of miles away, and every turn of the wheels brings her nearer Stark.

For three whole days Stark has wandered through the woods with his dog. Up hills, down dales, getting soaked in the rain and drying themselves in the sun. They chase rabbits, and Stark climbs trees, while Quick stands barking underneath. He has spent a lot of time just lying on his back, thinking hard. He returns to Wiss on Friday morning, his mind made up. He won't jump from that tower! Not that he couldn't work out some sort of safety device, but he refuses to waste his time on anything so stupid. That's not the way to become King of Katoren.

Although it is only seven o'clock, quite a lot of people are up and about and they all seem to be going in the direction of St Aloysius. Some have pillows under their arms, as if they have slept out on the pavement.

"Blast!" mutters Stark. "I suppose they want to be early so they can get a good view when I jump to my death!"

He had not intended to go to the Cathedral at all, but now he decides to go at ten o'clock to tell the people why he is refusing this challenge point-blank. But first he goes home.

Gervaas is making coffee. He rubs his hands together and seems in great spirits.

"The day of Task Four (a) has arrived," he says. "It will be a day long remembered in the history of Katoren."

"I'm not jumping!"

"No, but do go to the Cathedral in any case. The whole country has come to see you."

"I'll just go round and tell them why I'm refusing to jump."

"Right, you just tell them," says Uncle Gervaas cheerfully.

At half-past nine they leave the house, and by a quarter to ten they reach the square. It is crammed with people. But what is that near the tower? Some sort of building? What *are* the people throwing on it?

After he's published an angry editorial, "To blazes with Task Four (a)!", the editor of the *Katoren Herald* prints a special announcement asking all the citizens of Katoren to gather in St Aloysius Square with all the pillows and cushions they can lay their hands on. The editor is gratified to see the size of his paper's circulation when several thousand people turn up. They pile their pillows into an enormous mountain, which is so high that new arrivals have to climb the tower if they want to add more pillows to the top of the heap.

By the time Stark arrives, the pile is half as high as the tower itself. He suddenly realizes what's happening: the people actually *want* him to be King, and have come to help him. The crowd cheers as he starts to climb the tower. Uncle Gervaas stays down in the square, since he's too old to climb, but when Stark has climbed half way he hears someone coming up behind him. He turns, and there is Kim, flushed and breathless. She is carrying four pillows—her mother's, her father's, her own, and one from the bed in the spare room.

"Hello, Stark."

"KIM!"

He takes two of the pillows, and climbs with Kim to the highest gallery. Kim tosses the pillows down with a flourish. It still seems a long way down to the top of the pillow-mountain, but Stark grins.

"The pillows of all Katoren! What a soft landing! The old King used to say, 'When people light fireworks they honour you, but when they fluff out your pillows they love you.' I'm so glad you came, Kim. But listen, when I've jumped I'll be surrounded by all those people, and we might lose each other in the crowd. So go straight to my uncle's house. I'll meet you there as soon as I can."

"Promise you'll be careful, Stark."

"Don't worry. Everything will be fine."

He climbs on to the balcony and waves to the crowds below. Thousands of hands wave back, and thousands of voices cheer. Suddenly the crowd falls silent. The Ministers have arrived, walking in a solemn procession, three by three. They halt at the old King's statue. They may have changed his laws, but they'd never dare tamper with that statue. The Ministers have come to gauge the public's reaction. Things are much, much worse than they anticipated.

Stark, high above them, bows low to the Ministers. The people laugh. Then Stark straightens up, turns to give Kim a farewell kiss and, amidst a breathless hush, jumps from the tower. Straight as an arrow, then leaning slightly forward, his young body falls. Three seconds seem like three hours to Kim and Uncle Gervaas.

Then he lands on the pillows and disappears. The mountain topples over. Stark climbs out of the heap of fallen pillows. Amid the deafening cheers of the crowd he walks up to the Ministers.

"I hope you will give me my fifth task as soon as possible. I think you will agree we may dispense with task four (b), since task four (a) was really something of a joke. It was neither serious, nor honest, nor virtuous, nor diligent, nor orderly, nor hygienic. It was nothing but a soft option. Good morning."

He has just enough time to wave to Kim before the people lift him on to their shoulders and carry him through the town in a procession that lasts for hours. Finally he manages to escape from his admirers, and goes straight home, where he finds Kim and his uncle waiting for him.

Kim has twisted Uncle Gervaas right round her little finger. She's managed to find out every little detail about Stark's childhood. He's even let her see Stark's baby pictures, including one snapshot of Stark, age three, sitting naked on a fur rug. Only Stark's respect for his uncle's grey hairs stops him from committing mayhem.

Kim spends three happy days with Stark and his uncle. Kim has fallen madly in love and can't help showing it. Stark has fallen madly in love and doesn't even know it. Uncle Gervaas knows exactly what is going on, and says nothing, except to give Stark the latest news from the Palace.

The Ministers have fallen to quarrelling among themselves. They are frantically re-reading their file of letters, looking for a really ghastly and impossible task. They know they have three more chances, and the odds are against them. It's no use even trying on Five (a) or Six (b). They've seen what the people think of *that*.

"Well, that's their problem," is Stark's reaction. "Let's go and look at the sunset."

But the three idyllic days soon come to an end. Two letters arrive in the post. One is from Kim's father, who reminds his daughter that the schools haven't closed in honour of Stark and she'd better come home and pass her math exam. The other one is from the Council of Ministers, and contains a train ticket to Swindelburg, and a challenge to sort out the Swindelburg knobnose situation.

Kim sheds a few tears and goes home to Powdermill. Stark packs a few things in his week-end bag and goes off to complete his fifth task. Uncle Gervaas goes up to the Palace as usual, opens doors, brushes coats, and generally makes himself indispensible to the government of Katoren.

9

The Knob-Noses of Swindelburg

"Good morning, oh honourable Tara. I'm glad you have come."

"Good morning."

"It's my wife, Tara. This morning we noticed a little swelling. I'm afraid it's a case of . . ."

"I'll do the diagnosing."

"Of course, of course, Tara. I beg your pardon."

The little Mayor of Swindelburg takes the Tara's cap and gown and shows him into the bedroom, where his wife is lying in bed. She sits up when she sees the learned man, but he waves her back.

"Just lie there quietly, madam."

She obeys, glad that he has not noticed her shabby nightgown. The Tara takes a magnifying glass out of his case and examines her nose.

"*Stakare onissium plastaroze*," he mutters.

"What is your diagnosis, Tara?"

"*Plastaroze varietario cinearum*."

"Just so," says the Mayor, not a whit the wiser.

"You may fetch the ointment tonight. Apply it lightly twice a day. In a week it will be well again, so don't worry, madam, your little nose will be as straight as ever."

"Thank you very much, Tara."

The Tara pats her cheek, then the Mayor sees him out. A moment later he comes back, and nods encouragingly to his wife.

"Well, we caught it in time."

"Yes," she sighs.

"Come on, cheer up. You'll keep your nice, straight little nose, that's the most important thing."

"I *would* have liked you to have a piano. You were looking

81

forward to it so much. Now we'll have to start saving all over again."

"Don't worry about that, darling. Let's be glad we can pay him. It's fantastic he diagnosed it so quickly. Plastaroze and something."

"How clever they are, these Taras."

"Yes, they're wonderful. Did you hear the door-bell? I'll just have a look."

Stark is standing on the door-step. It has been a long journey to Swindelburg, on the western border of Katoren. As usual, his first action has been to seek out the Mayor, but he hasn't found it so easy this time. His first impression of Swindelburg is of small, shabby houses in need of a coat of paint, of badly-paved, dimly-lit streets, and of old, shaky buses—all-in-all a poverty-stricken place. But here and there amidst the shabbiness he has noticed a few fine, well-kept houses, like small castles. Two of these lie in the town square, so of course he takes one of them to belong to the Mayor—but no. He is directed to a much smaller, shabbier house near by. A timid little man in a worn old suit answers the door.

"May I speak to the Mayor?" he asks uncertainly.

"You *are* speaking to him," says the little man.

"You?" He has said it before he realizes how rude it sounds, but the little man doesn't seem to take offence.

"What can I do for you?" he asks in a very friendly way.

"I am Stark. I come from Wiss. I have a task . . ."

"You are Stark?" The little man pulls him inside with both hands, then, as if shocked by his boldness, takes Stark's shabby week-end bag, and places it on the staircase as if it were pure gold. He calls out excitedly that Stark has arrived, and shows him into the parlour, where they sit opposite each other on two very wobbly chairs.

"Mr Stark," he says, "I cannot believe that you have come to Swindelburg!"

"Please call me Stark, sir."

"What? Yes . . . all right, but what are you doing here?"

"I've come to cure your knob-noses. I must confess, I've never seen a knob-nose and I haven't the faintest idea what they are."

"What a happy creature you must be. Never seen a knob-nose! How is it possible?"

"Please tell me about them."

"Look, my wife is in bed with the beginning of a knob-nose. We call them K-noses. Would you mind if we talked in the bedroom? She'll be most anxious to make your acquaintance."

"Sure," agrees Stark.

A narrow, wooden staircase leads to the bedroom, where Stark is given the only chair. The Mayor sits on the bed.

"If you have a K-nose, I'd like to have one, too," remarks Stark, looking at Mrs Mayor's fine, straight profile.

"Oh my boy, don't say that! If my husband couldn't pay for the Tara's ointment, my nose would be as large and as red as a cabbage within a week."

The Mayor explains. For centuries, Swindelburg has been infested with a rare species of gnat, which breeds in the damp, peaty soil near the town. They are fond of landing on prominent places . . .

"Noses," says Stark.

"Exactly. The owner feels a violent prick and slaps his nose, mostly killing the gnat—but by that time it is too late. Soon the signs of a K-nose appear: a red dot, rising temperature, numbness of the nostrils. You know what happens then? The nose swells and swells into an awful-looking knob, then one of two things happens: either it bursts, and you die, or it stays as it is, and you have a disgusting-looking face."

"That sounds awful, sir."

"It is awful. Fortunately we have the Taras."

"What are the Taras?"

"They are the scholars of our town. You can tell them by the way they look, the way they hold their heads, how they wear their clothes. They know everything about K-noses. You realize, there are different sorts of gnats, all with their different poisons, so there are also different sorts of K-noses. We have the red-cabbage nose, the cauliflower-nose, the mushroom-nose, the onion-nose, the rhubarb-nose, and so on. These Taras know all about them all, they are the cleverest men in the world. They have developed medicines, which they are always improving, and with these they can now tackle the disease in its earliest stages."

"You seem very pleased with your Taras."

"They are geniuses," says the Mayor quietly. "They know everything. To question their judgement would be unthinkable."

"One thing I don't understand, sir. You say the Taras know all about this disease and can cure it. What is the problem, then? Why was I sent here?"

The Mayor bites his knuckles thoughtfully. "That's what I can't understand myself," he says at last.

"Don't be angry, my dearest," says his wife softly. "I wrote to Minister Kleen."

"*You* wrote? Why?"

"Stark," says the sick lady, "the K-noses are curable, it's true, but the medicines are so expensive, and so are the Taras' visits. We pay for each word they say, £1 a word. 'Good morning, madam' costs £3. That's what *I* object to. I know they have studied for years and have extraordinary talents, but, I mean . . . I thought . . . My husband is fond of music. We've been saving for a piano for more than fifteen years, and just when we nearly have enough, one of us gets a K-nose. Bang goes the money. Then I read about you, and I thought you might, well . . ."

"Might what?"

"You might find a way of getting rid of the gnats."

"Dearest, we can't do away with the gnats, it's the gnats' eggs which keep the peat strong, and but for them, Swindelburg would disappear from the earth. That's not what we want. I'm sorry, Stark, but I think you'd better go back and ask for another task. She meant well, but it's a shame to waste your valuable time."

"H'm. Would you mind if I stayed for a few more days?"

"Of course not. There's a spare bed in the attic, if you can make yourself comfortable there."

"Very kind of you, madam."

So once again Stark is a guest in the Mayor's household. He has never stayed in such a poor house before. A couple of horse-blankets are his bedding, and the meals consist of dry bread with goat's cheese, or potatoes and bacon. And to think the Mayor is one of the highest-paid people in the town! With the exception of the Taras, of course. Stark doesn't mind—there are no luxuries at his uncle's, either. The Mayor and his wife are kind, and that is the main thing.

That evening Stark goes with his host to collect the ointment. The heavy oak door is opened by a maid-servant. While they are waiting, Stark looks round. The heavy chandeliers, the costly carpets, all the richness, remind him of the town of Smog. He is not at all impressed by this grandeur. The Mayor turns his shabby hat nervously in his hands, his head slightly bent.

"This Tara seems to have a nice little income," observes Stark.

"Of course."

"It wouldn't be so nice for these Taras if we could do something about the knob-noses."

"Don't say that. They work night and day to keep us from suffering, no trouble is too much for them. If they had money worries they wouldn't be able to concentrate fully on their work. No, the Taras would be the first to welcome a solution."

"Maybe so. You know them better than I do."

Back home, Mrs Mayor's nose is carefully treated with the ointment, which smells of vinegar. After the frugal meal Stark asks if they have a book about the knob-disease. Apparently there isn't one. The Taras are afraid that people will try out different remedies for themselves, which could be disastrous. So they have refused to co-operate in writing a book. There are Taras and laymen, and nobody in between. Stark goes back to his attic and writes a letter to Kim, advising her to put a pile of maths books under her head at night, instead of the lost pillows. It may help to make up for the time she missed at school.

During the next few days the Mayor's wife recovers quickly, and Stark and Swindelburg get to know each other. The Swindelburgers are talkative and they enjoy meeting this famous young man. Stark notices quite a few K-noses—they really are horrible to look at. He meets a girl of Kim's age, with eyes nearly as beautiful as Kim's. She has a mushroom-nose.

"We were too late," she tells him sadly. "My father is rather mean with money, and when my nose began to swell he said it was only a wasp-bite, and didn't call the Tara in. A few days later I had a mushroom nose. We've had to pay so much for the treatments that we now live in the smallest house in the town."

"At least it didn't burst."

"Ah, but with such a nose, life isn't worth living. I'm only really at ease at the Society."

"Which society is that?"

"The C.O.N.K. Only K-noses can join. It's really a dramatic society. We like to act—it makes us feel normal."

"Is there no ointment that can cure you?"

"No."

"Even if you applied it very thickly for three weeks on end?"

"I don't think so. In any case, you'd need half a pail of the stuff, and it would cost more money than we've got."

"What's your name?"

"Irina."

"So long, then, Irina."

"So long, Stark."

He goes home and asks the Mayor's wife what she does with the left-over ointment. She says she throws it away. The Taras don't want it used by anyone else.

"May I have it?"

"I don't know, what will the Tara say?" she hesitates.

"Just give it to me. He may not ask about it."

He hides the little box in his attic and goes into town. By this time, word has got around that he is in Swindelburg, and that he is interested in K-noses. So he thinks it exceedingly strange that he cannot seem to meet a Tara.

When he rings the bell of a Tara's house it is always the same story: the Tara is too busy. He cannot speak to you. It's true, every Tara he passes in the street goes by very quickly, as if he had too much to do in too little time. Still . . . Unobserved, he follows the black-gowned men and rings the bells of the houses they have just left. In this way he sees for himself all the different kinds of K-noses. He also asks the patients to keep the left-over ointment for him, not to throw it away; and because he comes from Wiss and knows the Ministers, they promise to do so.

He discovers that the big building in the square, which he had thought was the town hall, belongs to the Society of Tarascience. The Society for the Treatment of K-noses holds its meetings there every Friday night.

"Do you think I could attend a meeting?" Stark asks the porter. The porter is quite shocked.

"Are you crazy? They won't have anything to do with laymen. In any case, you wouldn't understand anything they say."

"Then it wouldn't matter if I was there or not," replies Stark.

He doesn't care for these Taras, and can't share the townspeople's admiration for them.

During the week he collects twenty-two pots of left-over ointment. They all seem to be very similar in smell and consistency—only the colours are different. He mixes the contents of all the pots together into one pot, then goes to see Irina. As before, he has great difficulty in concealing his disgust at the sight of her nose.

"Look here, love," he manages to say, "here is one pot of K-ointment. Do me a favour and apply it for two nights, half a pot each time—a good lot of it, mind, not just a smear."

"Good heavens, Stark, this must have cost you a fortune!"

"I didn't pay a penny for it. *Will* you use it?"

"Are you sure it is the mushroom-ointment? It used to be green. This one is brownish."

"If you really want to know, this is a mixture of all the ointments—but dear Irina, let's face it, it could hardly make your nose look worse, could it?"

"You're right," says Irina thoughtfully. "It can't do much harm. All right, I'll do it."

"Now be sure to use plenty. There isn't much chance it will help, so don't expect great things. Please keep this to yourself, by the way."

Two days later, early in the morning, Irina pulls the bell of the Mayor's house. Convinced that the town is on fire, Stark rushes downstairs.

"It has gone down three millimetres!" she shouts.

Stark doesn't see any difference. It looks just the same to him.

"How do you know?" he says cautiously.

"I measured it." She adds shyly, "When you have a nose like mine, you know to a fraction how big it is. When I measured it this morning it was three millimetres less than the day before. I'm sure!"

Later that day Stark begs more left-over ointment, and gives half a pot to Irina. She treats her nose again that night, and again she notices a difference.

It is Friday again. Stark has thought things over, and says, "Irina, this Society of yours, C.O.N.K., do they have a Tara costume?"

"Of course we have. Why?"

"Will you trust me a little?"

"Stark, I'd do anything you say, even die."

"I don't need you to do that! Listen, I want to dress up as a Tara tonight—gown, cap, moustache, wrinkles, and all. Can you do it?"

"Yes, but what are you up to?"

"Don't ask questions, just bring what's necessary. Okay?"

"I'll do it."

Irina does a splendid job on him. That evening he looks exactly like a real Tara of about forty. But to look like one and to act like one are very different things. Fortunately Stark is rather bold. He holds his head high, puts up his finger with an air of command, and says, "Girl, hand me my cape."

"Yes, at once, Tara," she says timidly, then bursts out laughing. "Stark, that's marvellous! I really believed you were a Tara."

Resolutely he crosses the street and joins the Taras who are going into the Tarascience building. He is a little nervous, but says to himself, "After all, if these people are honest, it's not going to matter if I'm there. If they aren't honest . . ."

He hands his cape in at the cloakroom, and asks the attendant who the Chairman is that evening. He appears to be Tara of Hammerfield. Stark walks up to him and introduces himself as Tara of Rybridge, a small village some distance from the town.

"I hope you don't object to my attending your scientific meeting."

"Ha ha!" laughs Hammerfield. "You're joking. 'Scientific meeting', that's a good one. Make yourself comfortable, old man."

Stark is puzzled. What kind of joke has he made? It soon becomes clear.

Though he doesn't have the least little bit of scientific knowledge, a baby could tell that this is no scientific meeting. The

Taras just sit round, drinking one bottle after another—and it isn't lemonade. So as not to look different he joins a little group he has met on the way in.

"I didn't know Rybridge was big enough for a practice," remarks one. Can you make a living there?"

"Not a bad one, all things considered. In two years' time I'll have it made—provided the gnats are still around."

"Don't worry, the gnats will be faithful, all right. What will you have, whisky or vodka?"

"Vodka, please."

They pour him a drink. Stark takes a sip and immediately starts coughing. The Taras look at him in surprise.

"Caught a cold—ugh! ugh!—in my chest. This horrible climate."

"Terrible, isn't it?" says one of them. "I often suffer that way myself. Well, your health, old man." And he drains his glass in one draught.

Stark lifts his own glass and pretends to drink, but manages to empty it out into a nearby flower-pot.

"Well that does my chest no end of good."

There doesn't seem to be any formal meeting. The Taras sit together, cheerfully discussing their investments, property, the Tara Aeroplane Society, and the need to raise their scale of charges. Stark walks round unobtrusively, listening. He has not heard the word K-nose once. He decides to raise the subject himself.

"And how goes your practice, sir?" he asks a very tipsy, elderly gentleman.

"All right, thanks."

"I think I have identified a new kind of nose—Snake-nose, I call it," says Stark.

"Take purple, it's the only colour we haven't used yet."

"Purple?"

"Yes, purple ointment, but be careful to register it, both the colour and the name. Waiter! Double Scotch, please!" He gets his drink and promptly forgets the conversation.

Stark doesn't forget. A horrible suspicion has begun to form in his mind: do the Taras use the same ointment for each patient? A cold fury begins to grip him.

"I must control myself," he thinks. "I've got to find out everything now."

From time to time someone hands him another drink, and the rubber-plant gets another watering. He's surprised it doesn't start to sing. After a while its earth won't absorb any more alcohol. Towards two o'clock people start to leave, among them a man called Best, whom Stark has talked to.

"Oh, by the way, Best, I have someone coming early tomorrow to collect his mushroom-stuff, but I noticed as I came away that I've run out of it. Could you help me out?"

"I haven't got any either, but if you like to walk home with me we can make some up. I'm only two streets away."

"Very kind of you."

In Best's house they go straight to the laboratory.

"There's everything you need here. Just help yourself while I fetch a drink."

"The thing is, I'm so tipsy I'm afraid I'll drop everything," says Stark, with his famous presence of mind. "In my own lab—hic—I might manage, but in yours—hic—I don't know. Please help—hic, hic—me to do it."

"Well, well, well, so you've had one over the eight! All right, Tara helps Tara."

He takes a shovelful of peat, and sieves out the stones and twigs. He sprinkles it with flour, from a packet labelled "Self-raising flour, good for your pancakes", which seems to be ordinary baker's flour. Then he mixes in oil and mustard to make a paste. Stark sees some bottles of wine-vinegar, which remind him of the ointment's smell.

"Don't forget the vinegar," he says, in a voice hoarse with fury, which Best puts down to drunkenness.

"Of course not. It wouldn't work so well without it, and it would lack the characteristic smell. What was it? Mushroom-nose? Green, then." He turns to a row of little coloured bottles, picks out the green one, and adds a few drops.

"There! That's enough for twenty mushroom-noses. Here you are, colleague."

"Thank you so much," mutters Stark. "I'll do the same for you some time."

"Have another drink?"

"No, I must get home now. My car's still on the square, and I've rather a long way to go. Hic! Good-bye."

He hastens home. His first impulse is to wake the Mayor, but he decides to calm down a bit first. He is nearly shouting with rage, and too many people might hear. He pulls off the Tara-clothes, peels off the Tara-moustache, and washes his face. Then he falls into bed and dreams that all the Taras are lined up before him and he is flogging them all with a whip. The anger fades from his face. One might almost think that Stark is smiling in his sleep.

The Mayor simply won't believe him. His respect for the Taras is too deep, his fear of the disgusting K-noses too great. He keeps repeating, "It can't be true, it's impossible. You must be mistaken, Stark. The Taras are learned men. They are our benefactors. It's just impossible."

"Then what is this, sir? How do you think I got it?" He opens a large box of the green ointment.

"My boy, what abundance! Such a big box!"

"Nothing abundant about it. Look!" He takes a blob of the salve and throws it into the sink.

"What are you doing? Can't we use it? It's a sin to waste it like that!"

"Not a sin at all. For a few pence I can make as much as you want. For any type of K-nose. Believe me, sir, they're just a pack of charlatans."

"I just can't believe it, Stark."

"Actually, it is partly your own faults. You admired them and praised them so much, that they just got more and more conceited and pretentious. Well, I'm going out for a little, while you try and convince each other I'm right."

He takes the rest of the ointment to Irina.

"Here you are, enough for four days. When it's finished I can prepare as much more as you want."

"You? Prepare?"

"Yes, me. I'll explain later."

On the way home, with the little money he has, he buys

mustard, wine-vinegar, flour, and oil. At a gardener's he gets a sackful of peat.

"Is that the same kind the Taras buy?" he asks casually.

"Are you going to grow dahlias too? That's what the Taras seem to do with it," volunteers the gardener.

"Oh no, I'm going to make K-ointment with it, just like they do. Come to the market-place at two o'clock and I'll teach you. No more saving for Tara bills. Good-day." He leaves behind an astonished man.

Back at the Mayor's he hears them arguing.

"Lilliputians!" he calls out.

The small Mayor looks at him, quite at a loss.

"I'm sorry, sir, but I mean it. It's not your height, it's your mind. You're thinking too small to get at these Taras and do the town some good. Watch what I'm doing, watch closely." He puts the ingredients he has bought all together in a pail and stirs. He hasn't sifted the peat, so the mixture is a bit lumpy, but for the rest it is exactly the same as the ointment the Mayor and his wife know so well. "Now, if you want to be famous, go and get a few gnats from the marsh, then we'll go to the market-place. You let them sting you there, and I'll do the same. Then, in front of everyone I'll make the ointment and put it on our noses. After which, the Taras will be finished, and the knob-noses too.

"Yes do, darling!" says the Mayor's wife suddenly and firmly. The shabbily-dressed little Mayor straightens up, the light of battle in his eye.

"Now, at long last, I shall really be Mayor of Swindelburg," he says. "Up till now I have been too poor, and too scared of the Taras. Now things will change. My citizens will thrive. We will make new streets and build a bridge over the river. We will build a wonderful town hall and name it after you, my dear Stark. And now, my love, hand me my moth-net." Off he hurries to the marshes, his bald head shining in the sun.

After the demonstration in the market-place, the people don't know whether to be furious or glad. So they are both. They dance in the streets, shaking their fists at the Taras' houses. They even start throwing stones at the windows, but the Mayor puts a stop to that.

"Here's what we will do," he says, with a new authority. "For everything the Taras buy, we'll charge them treble-price. We'll go on doing that until they have to go and live in our old, decrepit houses, which we will soon be leaving. Just think, they won't be earning anything, so it won't take long. That's the way we'll deal with them, my friends, and no other way." The people pay attention to the Mayor and stop throwing stones. Instead, they dance round the Taras' houses, chanting, "Ha, ha, the Ta-ra!"

Stark makes another pailful of ointment for Irina. Her knob-nose is improving all the time, as are all the others. The cure works very slowly, but Stark is very hopeful that soon they will all be back to normal. Hasn't the old King said, "Even the thickest candle burns down in time"?

"Take care and stop using the ointment before your nose is gone!" Stark teases Irina.

The celebrations are still in full swing when Stark tells the Mayor and his wife that he has to leave.

"There's only one problem: how can I get a train ticket? I've spent all my money on flour, mustard, and oil."

"What a shame," says the Mayor. "We are so much in your debt, and I cannot even afford the money for your fare."

"Why darling," his wife says. "Don't you remember? We never paid the Tara for my treatment. So . . ."

"Oh no!" protests Stark. "Think of your piano."

"We'll get the piano, all right, now. How much is your fare?" Stark tells her, and with great pride she hands him the money. They go with him to the station, all three arm-in-arm, followed by a dancing crowd. The station is jam-packed with people, among them Irina. It is the first time she has dared to show her nose in public. It is still rather large, but definitely on the wane.

"I'll send you a photo when it's back to normal, Stark," she cries.

He waves to her and steps aboard. It is the first time he has returned to Wiss second-class, but that doesn't bother him. The train starts to move, and soon Swindelburg is lost in the darkness— but through the open window Stark hears a long echo of "Ha, ha, the Ta-ra!"

93

The Ministers Are Late

"Well, Stark, only two more!"

Gervaas sits in his little house behind the Palace, in very good spirits. He is now quite certain that his nephew will become King.

"Six and seven can just as well go wrong as one or two." Funny, with the first few tasks he was so sure of himself, but the more he succeeds, the·more he thinks of the possibility of failure. "I've been very lucky, Uncle Gervaas."

But Uncle Gervaas is convinced that Stark is a genius. It is hopeless to argue with him. So Stark re-reads the writings of the old King.

"A lighthouse with a strong light may fail when there is fog," he reads, "therefore it is wise not to put your lighthouse on the map. The captain will welcome its unexpected gleam in the dark, but a strong light dimmed by the mist will be useless, even dangerous."

"The King was a wise man," thinks Stark. How shall I ever follow in his footsteps?"

Two days later, on Thursday, as usual, he has to appear before the Ministers at ten o'clock. He is there five minutes early. On the stroke of ten Minister Watch strides through the hall and enters the Council chamber. He is followed ten minutes later by Minister Good, who nods kindly to Stark on his way in. It is twenty-five-past ten before Minister Kleen arrives. He takes off his rubbers and washes his hands ostentatiously, before going in. At twenty-five-to eleven Stark knocks on the door. Minister Good answers it, eyebrows raised.

"It's twenty-five-to eleven," says Stark.

"The devil it is! We'll call you when we need you!"

"I'm sorry for Minister Watch. He's sure to get a complex."

The door is slammed in his face. A few minutes later it opens

again and Minister Sure comes out, biting his handkerchief to keep from laughing. Last night his grandson said that Minister Kleen looked like a cake of soap, and he suddenly discovered his grandson is right!

At one minute to eleven the Minister of Honesty arrives. He has had a car crash, and it has taken him nearly an hour to convince the police that he really *wants* to be booked for careless driving.

Only Minister Rush is missing now. A cartful of sand has shed half its load in front of the Palace, and he is busy helping to get rid of the mess. At a quarter past eleven he comes dashing in. A moment later he is in the hall again, summoning Stark.

"Good morning, gentlemen, I hope you're in good health."

"A bit of a headache," replies Minister Watch. "Thank you."

The rest just nod.

Minister Sure is the spokesman.

"We hear from the Mayor of Swindelburg that you have dealt with the knob-noses. You have now completed five tasks, more or less successfully."

"Plus an (a)," Stark reminds him.

"Four (a) was just a joke."

"I am astonished to hear of jokes at the Ministry of Gravity."

"The policy of this Ministry is none of your affair."

"Well, I just thought I should know—just to prepare for the future."

A gnashing of teeth can be heard.

"Stark, my boy," says Minister Good, "I have a few things to say to you. My Ministry has prepared a White Paper on bad manners and forwardness. I suppose you know that you are rather forward?"

"Me? Forward?" Stark looks thunderstruck. "What does that mean?"

"Forwardness is lack of respect."

"Respect for whom?"

"For older and wiser people."

"Oh, but I have that. I respect my uncle very much."

"But you don't respect us. We are not as old as your uncle, but we could still be your father, even your grandfather."

"But you didn't just say 'older'."

Minister Good turns to his colleagues.

"You see, gentlemen? A hopeless case. My Ministry came to that conclusion."

"Excellencies, I don't want to hurt your feelings," says Stark, so I'll promise you one thing: when I am King you may be just as forward to me as I am to you now."

"You will never be King of Katoren," hisses Minister Kleen. "Do you believe in wizards?"

"Don't think so. Never seen one."

"You soon will. After long deliberation, we have come to the conclusion that you are not fit to be King. So we have chosen a task you will not be able to fulfil."

"Well, tell me what it is," says Stark encouragingly.

"You must destroy the wizard of Equilibrium."

"Seems an interesting job," says Stark.

"Wait till you have seen him," warns Minister Watch. "Here is your train ticket."

Stark looks at it. "Single ticket?" The Council is silent. "You do put all these towns to great expense. My last return journey cost the Mayor half a piano."

"There is no return from the Wizard of Equilibrium," says Good in a low voice. "Better stay at home with your uncle. He will soon be retiring. You may have his job."

"Very kind of you, exceedingly kind. I cannot accept such an offer, it is too much. You are so good, you bring tears to my eyes. How wonderful to have a Ministry of Virtue! I'll think of you every day in Equilibrium. Good morning."

With a speed that even Minister Rush could not achieve, he goes out, quite sickened by their hypocrisy.

"Good, I think you were too blatant about our intentions," says Sure.

"It is always better to tell the whole truth," says Strait.

"That's exactly what I did. Who can return from the Wizard of Equilibrium? When one tries to destroy him, one destroys oneself."

They all shake their heads solemnly. What a miserable sight. Is there not even a twinge of concern for their young challenger in these six cold hearts?

II

The Wizard of Equilibrium

At first sight, Equilibrium does not seem greatly affected by its Wizard. Stark walks out of the station into a cheerful, prosperous town. Fountains throw thousands of water-diamonds into the air. Gaily-painted tram-cars move in all directions, bells clanging. The terraces are crowded with people enjoying their beer in the sun. What a contrast to the shabbiness of Swindelburg!

Stark decides to have a cool drink on the terrace—his uncle has given him a little money. Soon he gets talking to a young man of about his own age, called Michael. Michael is very happy here in the mountains. The climate is wonderful. One can ski, climb, and walk, and working conditions are good—full employment for everyone and high wages. Then there are excursions every so often, and no other town in Katoren has so many shows, circuses, and amusement parks.

"A marvellous town to live in," he sums up.

"No problems?"

"Not that I know of."

"I've heard talk of a wizard. Is he a problem?"

"Sh! We don't mention him. Let's change the subject. Tell me about Wiss."

It is still early, so Stark strolls about for a while in the sun, before going to seek out the Mayor. He is struck by the number of dogs he sees being walked, mostly on the leash, by very elegant owners. To his sorrow, he also sees an accident. An old man is hit by a car. He lies motionless on the pavement, bleeding profusely. An ambulance arrives within five minutes. Stark is puzzled to see that no one passing by is paying the slightest attention. He also wonders why the stretcher-bearers screen off the patient and the car so quickly.

Apart from that, everything seems very pleasant and cheerful.

Then he notices a woman catching up with her friend and tapping her on the shoulder. The friend's reaction is hardly normal: she sways and almost faints. Not a very important incident, and a moment later they walk on together, talking cheerfully; but Stark has been startled by the friend's terror. He can't forget her tense, drawn face.

Presently he arrives at an elegant town hall, and finds the Mayor's house next door. A young girl answers his ring.

"Is the Mayor at home? I come from Wiss. My name is Stark."

"*The* Stark? The Stark of the Dragon, the pomegrenades, and St Aloysius . . .?"

Stark smiles. "That's the one."

"Please come in. Madam will be here in a minute."

"I can go to the town hall, if the Mayor is there."

"No, she will be back any minute now."

"She? Is the Mayor of this town a woman?"

"Of course. Didn't you know?"

He is put into a chair and given a cup of tea and a bun. The girl can't stop looking at him. Fortunately, the Mayor soon comes in, a dignified figure in a long black dress with a little white collar. She has grey hair and a strange look of calm. She welcomes Stark warmly and sends the girl to the kitchen.

"So the Ministers sent you after all," she says in a low, musical voice.

"Yes, Madam Mayor. But why 'after all'?"

About a month ago, I received a letter from Minister Good, asking about our troubles with . . . er . . . our difficulties, and he suggested sending you. I advised him not to."

"Why?"

"Because I had followed your success in the papers, and I didn't think it right that you should fail at a task that is beyond the power of any human being, even you—and you are a very able young man, even though you look just like any ordinary boy."

"Thank you."

"And now you are here, after all."

"I don't wish to be impolite, but every other Mayor, too, has told me that his problem is insoluble, and yet . . ."

"And yet, you have found a solution. Do you know why?"

98

"I think", says Stark thoughtfully, "it's because I came fresh to these problems. The townspeople were too close to them to see the solution. I started from the idea that there must be ten different solutions. Also, I had luck on my side. Perhaps that's because I was born on the day of the old King's death. I am the oldest person in Katoren not to have known him."

"It's unbelievable. Only eighteen!" She shakes her head. "Well, you can stay here for the night and travel back tomorrow. I'll give you a letter for the Ministers, and they'll give you a different task."

Stark shakes his head. "I stay here till my task is done. You can't send me away. If you do, I'll come back in disguise. I've something to do here."

"Oh, my boy, what can I say?"

"You can tell me who this Wizard is."

Silence. Calmly she pours out more tea.

At last, "I'll tell you," she says wearily.

"Every night an old man comes to our town and rings a doorbell, just one. It could be the same one twice in a week or not once in a hundred years, no one can tell. Pantar, they call him, just an ordinary old man begging alms from a different house each night —nothing very special in that, is there?"

She pauses. Stark senses the effort she is making to continue.

"You give him something—but it's not right, not enough. It has to be a real sacrifice, something you will miss sorely."

"And if not?"

"Listen, suppose you were well-off and gave him £100, you'd forget about it next day. He takes it, but he knows—he feels, it is not any real sacrifice, even if you have tears in your eyes and pretend it is. He will then walk in and take your most precious possession—your total savings, your photograph album, your pet, your wedding dress, or . . . or something worse."

"And if you resist?"

People say he lifts his little finger and changes you into a clock; but everyone is much too upset to resist. There *is* no resistance against Pantar. And now, will you leave, Stark?"

Stark shakes his head. The grey lady sighs deeply.

"This evening I'll tell you something I have not talked about for twenty years. Then you'll leave, I am sure. Go and take a walk in the park, just now. I'll have a room arranged for you, then send the servant away and do the cooking myself. Dinner at six-thirty. All right?''

"Very kind of you, ma'am.''

He views the town with different eyes, now. 16, Minerva Lane: has Pantar been there? What did they give him? 72, Minerva Lane, Palfener and Koatchman, Lawyers: what would they give Pantar if he came to their homes tonight? What would he himself give? His letters from Kim? His dog? The old King's writings? His father's old trowel?

Obediently he is back at half-past six sharp. They dine together very cosily, Stark eating two platefuls, the Mayor only a few bites. They do the washing-up together as if they were mother and son. Then the hostess makes coffee and they sit opposite each other. A silence falls over the room.

This is the story of the Lady Mayor of Equilibrium.

For twenty years she lived with her husband, the rich young Mayor, in this very house. Ivy surrounded the windows, and the rooms were filled with flowers. They had one child, a little girl, who was their constant joy and delight. How happy she was looking after her, how gaily she sang to her! Her husband had four great passions: his beautiful wife, his little daughter, his Mayor-ship, and his stamp collection, on which he spent much of his leisure. There was no happier family in the whole of Equilibrium, or for miles around.

One night the bell rang. The Mayor answered the door—and there stood Pantar, old and decrepit, begging a gift. They had always known it could happen, but had never let it worry them.

"All right, old man," said the Mayor, "Just one moment." He went up to his room and fetched all his savings, in a small chest. "Here you are, that is every penny we possess. You may keep it all."

The old man took the chest under his arm, then shook his head very slowly. Without a word he walked past the Mayor, through the corridor, and into the room where his wife was busy with the child. And he took the little girl. Husband and wife looked on, stunned with horror, as he took her and disappeared into the night.

"My fault!" the Mayor exclaimed in anguish. "I cared nothing for the money. If it had been ten times as much, I would not have lost a moment's sleep. My stamp collection, I should have given him that!" He took all his five thick books full of stamps and threw them into the fire. "I am damned for all eternity!" he cried, and turning, fell dead from a heart attack.

There is not much more to tell. After losing child, husband, money, and stamp collection within ten minutes, her hair turned grey and the smile left her face for ever. She became Mayor in her husband's place, but had no desire for any possessions. She was the only person in Equilibrium who did not fear Pantar, for she had nothing to lose; but that was small consolation.

"And now," she concludes dully, "will you go away to-morrow?"

Stark takes her thin hand in his.

"Now I am quite sure I must stay."

Every day in the Equilibrium morning paper, beneath the weather forecast, a single address is printed. It is the house Pantar has visited the previous night. Stark talks to the victims. The circumstances are always quite different. One man grieves for his dog.

"Did you give him the dog, or did he take it?"

"We gave it, of course. That was why we got him in the first place."

"You mean . . .?"

"But of course. Why do you think there are so many dogs in Equilibrium? Everybody gets a dog and tries to become attached to it, then they have something to give away if the bell is rung. If you don't care for the animal, you might as well get rid of it, for it won't do you any good."

"Has Pantar been to you before?"

"No, only to my parents, about thirty years ago. Please excuse me now, I must go and buy a new dog."

An old, retired baker is really sad. He has given Pantar half his savings, and now he must go and live in a smaller house.

"Wasn't it dangerous to give him money?"

"No. I am rather thrifty, and I have worked hard and saved all my life. I am really distressed to lose it."

"You always knew this might happen. Why didn't you leave Equilibrium?"

"Why do people live near volcanos? Equilibrium is my home, it's a good town, there's good money to be earned here. Also, the chances of him coming are quite small, perhaps once in a lifetime. You never know, though. He has visited my neighbour three times in five years. I had thought of marrying her, but not now— Pantar finds her too attractive!"

"Well, sir, good luck with your removal."

One day Stark thinks he has come to the wrong address, 1, Hercules Lane, for a gay party seems to be going on. A fat man, in high spirits, welcomes him with a gold-toothed grin, into a parlour which boasts polished furniture and a silver tea-service.

"Never had such a laugh," he booms. "All my life I've dreaded a visit from the old man, and sweated at the thought of losing so much money—I've a prosperous business. When the bell rang yesterday evening I never thought of Pantar, neither did my wife. Nicolette, our daughter, went to the door. She's five. She had an old, shabby doll in her arms, such a doll!—straw coming out of one leg, and a hole in its head. My wife and I hear an old man's voice asking for alms, and Nicolette saying 'What do you mean?'

'I want you to give me something', he says. We just sit there rigid with fright, waiting for her to come and ask us about it. But what does the child do? She says, 'You look very lonely. You may have my doll, she is a darling doll.' We think, 'That's done it, now he'll take what he really wants.'

"But what does he do? He just says, 'Thank you, my child', and we hear the door close. Nicolette comes in, looking at her empty arms. 'I have given away my doll', she says, and starts to cry. 'My child', I tell her, 'you'll get ten dolls from me, much nicer ones too'. And I kept my word. I went straight to the shops, and just look at these."

With all the weight of his fat smugness he pushes Stark into the back room, where Nicolette is sitting unhappily, surrounded by ten huge dolls that can walk and talk and say "Mama". Stark strokes her hair gently, and escapes from the house as quickly as he can.

How can he ever meet Pantar? He is always a night and a day

102

behind him. He has now been in Equilibrium for over a week.

The Lady Mayor is enjoying his visit. It is a pleasure to cook for someone who likes his food; and he says what he thinks and shows feeling and understanding, both to her and to the people he visits. He lacks a mother, and she lacks a child. They understand each other very well. Younger than her daughter would have been, and yet he has met all these challenges with such success! Not that he boasts, he seems to take them as a matter of course—but she sees very clearly that his solutions have all shown imagination and courage.

It is Saturday evening. The autumn storms have come, and they sit together comfortably in front of the stove. It is almost home-like in the dreary, sparsely-furnished house. Stark is imitating all the Ministers for the Mayor's benefit, when the bell rings.

"Now who could that be, so late at night?" She does not think of Pantar, he holds no terror for her. She goes to the hall and opens the door. There on the steps he stands, the Wizard of Equilibrium, his shabby collar turned up.

"I come to ask you for a gift," he says. Her heart turns cold as ice—not from fear, but from fearful memory.

"I have nothing that is worth anything," she says, giving him her purse. He puts it in his pocket, shakes his head, just as he did twenty years ago, and walks past her into the room.

"That boy," he says. "He is not grown up, he is in your house, so he is yours. I'll take him."

She faints.

"Come, boy," says Pantar.

"I don't know you, but I'm not afraid of you."

"I can change you into a clock, but then I'd have to carry you, and I'd rather you walked."

"I'll walk if you allow me to help this lady."

"Five minutes."

With some difficulty Stark heaves her on to the couch. He sprays lavender water on a handkerchief and holds it to her nose. When she starts to move and show signs of coming round, he puts on his coat and follows Pantar. The Wizard signs to the boy to sit in the old bicycle-trailer which stands in front of the door. The old man gets stiffly into the seat and starts pedalling.

It is a hard job. They make little headway against the strong gusts of wind. Stark sits on this peculiar contraption, knees drawn up and coat collar tightly round his neck, and sees the lights of the town fade slowly into the distance. They are going south, travelling along a winding, narrow path. The enormous rocks on each side of it become weirder in shape the farther they travel. Turning round, he sees how little strength the old man has. He cups his hands and shouts, "Shall I cycle for a bit?"

Pantar stops. Stark jumps down.

"Whoever threatens me shall at once change into a clock," says the Wizard in a monotonous voice. Stark nods. He waits while the old man manoeuvres himself into the tiny trailer, then jumps on to the seat. They go forward much more quickly now. Pantar indicates the way with a wave of his hand. Fortunately there is a little moonlight, otherwise Stark could not pick out the narrow pathway through the crags and boulders, or avoid the deep ravines. At length Pantar points to the right. There seems to be a mountain blocking their way, but as Stark steers hesitatingly towards it, the brushwood parts, and they ride deep into a dark cave in the heart of the mountain. It is a relief to be out of the wind, but it is pitch black.

"Straight on . . . stop."

They are at the foot of a stone stairway, dimly lit from above. The old man gets out and signs to Stark to follow him up the flight of steps, which are hewn out of the rock. At the top is a stone chamber. The light comes from a big fire burning in a hole in the middle of its floor, guarded by a low wall. For the rest, there is a bed, a couple of old chairs, a table and a tall cupboard.

Pantar goes up to the fire straight away and warms his hands.

Forthright as ever, Stark says, "What an awful job for an old man like you, to make that journey into Equilibrium every night."

"Come and stand near the fire," says the old man, "here, where there is an opening in the wall." It is the very place where a little push could topple someone into the heart of the fire.

"Why do you want me to stand there?"

"Never mind. I'll change you into a clock first, and you won't notice a thing."

"Oh, won't I?"

Feverishly he thinks of a way out. Apparently the old man throws his "gifts" into the fire: easy with a wallet of money, but with a heavy "gift" like Stark, Pantar has to have it near the fire, so as not to carry it. Stark takes a few steps forward, as if obeying the Wizard. Then suddenly he jumps on to a chair, from there to the table, and from the table to the top of the tall cupboard.

"Don't change me into a clock," he calls. "You would break your neck if you had to fetch me down."

The grey Wizard looks annoyed.

"What do you want? Do you think you can withstand me?"

"No, Pantar, but I want to talk to you before you throw me in the fire."

"There is nothing to talk about."

"Please, I beg you. I want to know why I have to die."

Pantar hesitates.

"Well, all right, but only because you drove the trailer for me. Come down and sit in the chair."

None too sure that he can trust the old man, Stark climbs down and takes off his coat. Then he takes a seat opposite the disgruntled wizard, who still shivers with cold, in spite of the fire.

"No one has ever heard my story," he begins, "the story of the Wizard and the town of Equilibrium. To you alone, this one time, will I tell it tonight."

He takes a piece of crystal from a shelf and puts it on the table in front of Stark.

"Look into that."

Stark looks. A pair of scales appears. On one scale he sees the town of Equilibrium, built just above a deep hole. If the scale were not kept balanced, the whole town would disappear into the void. He looks at the other scale. What keeps the town in balance is only a fire, one small fire. It is this very fire in the Wizard's stone chamber.

"For five hundred years I have lived in this mountain, and my father for five hundred years before me. It was his duty—as now it is mine—to keep the fire burning, for if it ever goes out, the town and all its inhabitants will disappear from the earth. But this is no ordinary fire. Its only fuel is gifts, and only gifts that involve some hardship have the right weight to keep the town in balance. It is these sacrifices alone which keep the fire burning.

"The fire must be fed every day. That is my task. Every single day for five hundred years, to save the town, I have taken something from somebody that he would rather have kept. To help me in this, my father taught me two tricks: first, I can sense if the gift is a real sacrifice, or not; and the other is that if I am threatened by any person or any thing, I can change them into a clock. With the aid of these two tricks I can carry out my appointed task.

"But now I am growing old. I have no son. I can keep on perhaps for five more years, perhaps thirty; but sooner or later the end will come. Then Equilibrium will sink into the ground, and the spot where it stood will be a gaping void."

For a long time they sit there in silence. Then Pantar says wearily, "So now you know the secret of Equilibrium. Please stand near the fire."

"Will the fire burn on nothing else? Only sacrifices?"

"Only sacrifices. They need not be voluntary—well, you know that yourself. If one person were to sacrifice his life of his own free will, however, the fire would burn for a hundred times a thousand years. But my father never came across such a person, and neither have I. Come now, boy. Stand near the fire."

"Just one moment. Are you saying that if I jump into the fire of my own free will, it will burn for all these years?"

"Of course not. I forced you to come, you cannot call that free will."

"Pantar, let me go. I'll be back tomorrow evening and throw myself willingly into the fire."

The old man laughs—a short, cheerless sound.

"Tomorrow night you will be hundreds of miles from here."

"You might at least try it. Even if I were to escape, what would it matter, just one sacrifice against so many thousands?"

"Impossible. If the fire is not fed tonight, it will die."

"Then would you be prepared to go to Equilibrium again tonight, to get another gift, just on the chance, the small chance, that I will come back tomorrow night and you will never have to go again?"

"I have no strength to do so."

"I'll drive the trailer for you—and ride it back again, too. Oh please, Pantar, say you'll come."

The old man stares at the boy for a long time. Then he gets up rather shakily and puts on his shabby coat.

Huddled down inside his coat, Stark has been waiting at the edge of the town for almost an hour now. With the wind behind them, the ride back to town had been easy.

"1, Hercules Lane, the address you were at a few days ago," he whispers, as the Wizard rides stiffly away.

The journey back will be more difficult. At last he hears the soft, grinding sound of the trailer. The old man looks pale and exhausted. Even this little journey into the town has been too much for him.

For all he is glad of the exercise to warm him, Stark, too, is tired by the time they reach the cave. The journey was like a nightmare: he, Stark, pedalling that ridiculous vehicle, with a shivering Wizard as passenger, black clouds obscuring the moonlight, wild winds howling all around. Any normal wizard would just say, "Hocus pocus, fft! . . . home!" but not Pantar. Is Pantar real? He remembers the eyes of the Lady Mayor. Yes, Pantar is real.

Upstairs in the stone chamber, Pantar is taking a bundle of papers from his pocket.

"The man with the gold teeth," he says. "He was not startled at all. He sends his child to me, half-asleep, an expensive doll in each arm. 'I am to give you these, my father says—and please, will you give me back my old doll?' Then I went to fat gold-tooth's desk and took at least half his fortune. His eyes popped so far out of his head, he could see his toes for the first time in years."

Stark grins, but his thoughts are elsewhere.

"Take, oh fire, this small sacrifice," chants Pantar dutifully, and throws the papers on the fire. Then he gets a bundle of old blankets out of the cupboard and throws them at Stark's feet.

"Just make a corner for yourself on the floor."

He himself drops on to the shaky bed, clothes and all, pulls the blankets up to his nose, and starts to snore.

Wide awake in his corner, Stark stares into the flames that leap over the low wall. Slowly fear wells up in him. Where will he find courage to throw himself in the fire?

In the morning he is away at first light, wandering through the mountains which circle Pantar's cave. Around midday, it occurs to him that he has eaten nothing since the evening before. His stomach is full of fear, not hunger. He thinks of a thousand reasons to run away. Is the town really in such danger, or is it only the fantasy of a crazy old man? He has already completed five tasks. Is his duty to stay alive and become King of Katoren? Could he not do more for Katoren that way, rather than die for a handful of people in one town? Suppose he went back to the Mayor—how glad she would be to see him! She would write to the Ministers saying he had solved the problem: they would know no different until after he had become King. Then again, was he right in trying to stop these sacrifices? It is better to give than to receive. Should he prevent this daily offering? Sacrifice is good for the soul.

He eats a few blackberries. They taste bitter. Ah, he knows quite well he is deceiving himself. These forced sacrifices don't make Equilibrium one whit better—on the contrary, the people grow more and more frightened and unhappy. If they made gifts of their own, free will . . . then perhaps. And his kingship? If he offers his own life, he will not be King—and yet, in his heart of hearts, he knows that if he does not make this sacrifice, he is not worthy to be King.

The sun climbs inexorably to its zenith, then sinks lower and lower towards the horizon in the west. Soon it will disappear, and the end of the day will have come. And still Stark wrestles with his problem. It is a greater trial of strength than Minister Good, for all his dire forebodings, could have known.

Not for one moment does Pantar believe the boy will come back, and at ten o'clock he puts on his coat to go to the town, grumbling to himself. His rheumatism has grown worse with sitting hunched up in the trailer. Somehow, he can't think too badly of Stark. He wants this sympathetic boy, the only person who has really talked to him in all these years, to live and be free. Slowly he hobbles down the stone steps.

Stark is sitting at the bottom. Pantar clutches his shoulder to save himself from falling. Old man and boy stand trembling together, the one with cold, the other with fear.

"Why didn't you escape?" murmurs Pantar reproachfully.

"Let's go up. You need not go to town any more."

With no further word they mount the steps. In the chamber they both take off their coats.

"Sit down, please, for a moment," says the old man. "There is time enough. Tell me why you want to do this."

"Let's not talk about it. In five minutes my courage will have gone. What are the words I must speak?"

"Wait, sit down there. You are so young—young people want to live," says the Wizard abruptly. "I must know why you want to die."

"I do not want to die," says Stark, his voice choked, "but those people of Equilibrium want to live too. There are thousands of them, and only one of me."

"Those cold creatures? They think only of themselves. To them I'm the nasty Wizard who takes away their things. Nobody ever asked me why I needed them. They give the smallest thing they think they can get away with, they hate me and swear at me. You're crazy to trouble about them."

"Why have you troubled with this thankless task? Why not let the town just sink into the void?"

The old man gets up. He shakes the locks of his grey hair over his eyes. Now he really looks like a dangerous wizard. He walks up to the fire and clenches his fist at the flames.

"Many a time I decided to stop, but their red tongues demanded food, told me in a thousand ways that they would take the townspeople—those villains who dance in the streets, sit in the sun and live as if there were no death and destruction. Why did I do it? Because I am crazy, as crazy as you are. But I am old and you are young. I have a right to be crazy, but you have not. You must use your good sense. So dance in the streets, sit in the sun, and think that the world is yours—that is your right. I claim my right to be crazy. Oh fire, take this little offering!"

With a frenzied cry, Pantar throws himself into the flames and disappears.

Stark remains in the cave for another day and a half, as a kind of mourning for Pantar.

In the evening he looks at the fire. Will it go on burning? It looks the same as ever. The secrets of the old man have vanished with him into the fire.

Stark decides that, before he leaves, everything belonging to Pantar should also vanish. He pulls the old trailer up the stone stairway and throws it into the fire. The bed and the chairs follow, then the cupboard, which he has to kick to pieces. All that is left is an empty cave, in which a small crater burns.

"Rest in peace, Pantar," says Stark. "Who you were I shall never know, but in your strange heart there was love for this wicked world. I promise that never will my lips tell what I know of you."

Strange rumours run through the town. Stark has been taken by Pantar. The Mayor reported it to the local paper. Then the inhabitant of 1, Hercules Lane maintains that he, too, has had a visit. Most astonishing of all, on Sunday there is no report from anyone of a visit. Nor on Monday. Stark's incredible powers are well-known. Could it possibly be . . .?

About midday Stark arrives at the Mayor's house. The little servant girl thinks he is a ghost, and cries out in fright.

"Don't panic, my child," says Stark. "Is the Mayor at home?"

She is not in.

"Have you something I could eat? I'm nearly fainting from hunger."

That helps to calm the girl. Ghosts don't eat. Stark gets through everything in the bread-bin with astonishing speed. While he is doing so, the girl rings the town hall. Although she is presiding over a meeting, the Mayor comes home straight away, leaving her deputy in charge. When she sees Stark she discovers she can still cry. She kisses his forehead and tells the ceiling that this is her first happy day in twenty years. When they are calmer and Stark has eaten his fill, she wants to know how he managed to get back from Pantar.

"I promised to tell nobody," he says, "not even you ("especially not you!" he thought); but I can tell you this much: Pantar will never come to Equilibrium again. People can be sure of that."

"He did not come last night, nor the night before."

"He'll never come back, but please don't ask my why."

"You are a strange boy, Stark. Soon you'll be King of Katoren. This was your sixth task, wasn't it?"

"The sixth, yes. Only one more left."

"I think Katoren will have a glorious future with you as King. I'll serve you faithfully."

"Oh, don't speak like that. We'll all work together for the good of the people, you here, me in Wiss. It will be nice to know that I have a special friend in Equilibrium—if I may call you that?"

She nods. "Yes, to be sure you may. Now, what can I do for you at present, Stark?"

"I have three wishes. First, will you write to the Ministers that the Wizard of Equilibrium has disappeared? Second, will you buy me a ticket to Wiss? Thirdly . . . it is not really a wish, but would you consider building a statue for Pantar?"

"A statue for that . . . that . . . !"

"He did many good things for your town, but above all . . . that statue will remind people from time to time that there is such a thing as sacrifice—of their own free will, I mean."

"We'll see, Stark. Now I'll take you to the station. You must get back to Wiss as soon as possible, Katoren needs its new King. I'll write to the Ministers, and of course I will buy your ticket."

When they come out of the house, there is a crowd waiting.

"Is he dead?" they call.

"He won't come any more, ever."

"What did you do to him?"

"He did something to me. I must go. Good-bye."

At last Stark escapes into the train. Of all the people on the platform he sees only the Mayor. Her eyes are full of tears. She takes a handkerchief from her bag, but uses it to wave to him. The little white square is soon lost to sight, but even back in Wiss he can still see her.

12

A Meeting in the Park

Minister Sure stands in front of the mirror, touching up his hair with dye. He notices one of his few, precious hairs clinging to the brush. Even without that he is in a bad temper. Yesterday's evening papers have reported feasting in Equilibrium, and there is no need for him to read more than the headlines to know what that means. The *Katoren Herald* has even commented that these feasts will be good practice for the coronation festivities.

Minister Sure feels exhausted. He knows that none of the Ministers can possibly think of a task more difficult than this last one. Moreover, he is beginning to doubt his own ability to be Minister of Gravity. Yesterday his grandson made him laugh again, out loud—fortunately no one else was there. (What did the little rascal say? What is the difference between Minister Rush and a car? One runs on petrol, the other just runs.) He warns his wife to go about her household duties solemnly and soberly, and leaves for the Palace.

On the way he meets his colleague Watch. He, too, looks troubled. His shoelace has broken, and putting in a new one has cost him seventy seconds.

"Watch," says Minister Sure, "let's take a stroll round the park."

Mr Watch is shocked at the idea. "I have to be in my office by nine," he says.

"To do what?"

"First I have to wind the clocks, then turn all the hourglasses. At ten o'clock I must check that everyone is in."

"Just skip it all for once."

"Then the daily lists won't check, then the weekly lists will be wrong, and the monthly ones, and the annual ones." The poor man's stomach aches at the idea.

"And if you sprained your ankle? What would happen then? Come on, old man, we're going to the park."

Minister Good has recited the twelve golden rules of virtue with his family, and is ready to go to his Ministry. He sees that it is a fine day. The morning sun makes the autumn trees look glorious. He is just home from the country, and has read in all the papers of Stark's success in Equilibrium. Deep down it begins to dawn on him that his lectures on virtue do much less good than this boy's activities. He doesn't feel like going to his dull Ministry; he'd rather take a walk. So he gives Minister Strait a ring.

"Good here. You're still at home, I gather."

"I'm just leaving."

"Listen, I feel like a walk in the park. I'll come and fetch you."

"I don't think . . . why yes, I'd like that," says Minister Strait. After all, he has plenty of time to spare.

"I'll be round right away."

Minister Strait, too, is sad this morning. He has found his wife lying to him. When he asked her about her headache, she said she was all right, but a moment later he saw her take some aspirins. He sighs. How little success he and his Ministry have had. Even his colleagues tell small lies—except for Good, who really tries. He looks forward to a walk with his colleague.

Ministers Rush and Kleen don't get on too well together—Kleen is always holding up the impatient Rush while he washes his hands. They keep out of each other's way as much as possible, but this morning Rush suddenly decides to call on his colleague. He has read the news about Stark, and wants to take action immediately. (Minister Kleen has no telephone. A thing like that against one's ear? Terribly unhygienic!)

They walk towards the park together. It isn't easy for either of them. Rush tries to walk slowly, which he hates doing, while Kleen races as fast as he can, coughing and gasping for breath. Half-way round the park, he suggests going to look and see if the swans have been put in their winter quarters yet.

"I'll just run and look," says Rush, and trots off. Kleen sits thankfully down on a bench, after spreading his handkerchief on it. He has a whole five minutes of rest, before Rush comes dashing back.

"The swans are there, but not only the swans, just come and look."

And so it happens that all the Ministers of Katoren are to be seen sitting together in the sun, on a bench in the park, during working hours—a memorable morning indeed.

"I don't think we should all be seen here together," ventures Minister Good.

"I quite agree," says Minister Sure. "Parks are the breeding-grounds of idleness and gaiety."

"The walk wasn't on *my* schedule," complains Minister Watch.

"It isn't right, because others are working," is Minister Strait's contribution.

"All those filthy insects crawling about," splutters Minister Kleen.

"And we're not doing a thing," points out Minister Rush.

But they stay where they are. The autumn sun shines down on their bald heads—and that, to some people in this world, is a good feeling.

"Stark," mutters Minister Sure.

The others nod.

"He's done it again. I give in, you cannot beat that boy."

The others nod again. They have reached the same conclusion.

"I suggest that we make the last task an easy one," says Sure.

Is it the influence of the sun? Or of meeting in the open air? Or the idea that the future King might seek his revenge on them? They discuss the last task—it mustn't be too easy. They decide that Stark must go and sit on the Stone Seat of Stillwood.

The Fateful Seat

13

The little village of Stillwood lies ten miles from Wiss. It consists of a tiny village square with a few houses around it, a small church, and an inn. Only a handful of old people live there. The younger generation has long since left for the city.

It is in this sleepy place that Stark must fulfil his last task. On Sunday morning he pumps up the tyres of Uncle Gervaas's old bike, and sets off. The weather is fine, and he has had some cycling-practice in Equilibrium. He thinks back to his home-coming a few days ago. It was much quieter this time. The journalists are cross with Stark for refusing to give them any details, so, apart from the usual headlines, there has been very little fuss about the sixth task.

"The Stone Seat of Stillwood." Uncle Gervaas remembered vaguely that someone, a long time ago, had fallen off it.

"Take care," he had said. "The Ministers may have been nicer to you this time, but I don't trust them an inch."

Stark smiles as he thinks of his dear old uncle. He sees a steeple in the distance—that must be Stillwood. He wonders what the problem is about sitting on a stone seat. Ten minutes later he realizes that he has very nearly passed through the village without noticing it, it is so small.

He dismounts in the empty little square, and props his bike against a lime tree. There, right in front of him, is the Stone Seat, fenced around with iron spikes and barbed wire. It looks like a huge, old-fashioned chair, built with enormous boulders. Attached to one side is a wooden board, warped by wind and rain, with some lettering on it—once gold, perhaps, but now dingy and half worn away. With some difficulty Stark deciphers the words.

Whoever climbs this chair
Is sure to die;

So give away your goods
And don't ask why.

"Thanks for the invitation," he grins. "I have no goods, so as to that I could go and sit on it—but I could still die, I suppose, and I'd rather not."

Apart from that, there seems to be nothing dangerous about this chair. It's just a heap of boulders put together rather haphazardly. An ugly thing, really, but certainly solid enough. Well-secured, too, he decides, after testing the heavy, rusted padlock of the gate in the fence.

He decides to leave the chair to itself for a while, and go and get a drink at the little inn—good old Uncle Gervaas has once again given him a little pocket-money. The inn is like any other village inn in the early afternoon. There are a few small, plastic-covered tables, some wooden chairs, and a bar with shining beer-taps—everyone knows this sort of place. Stark shouts a few times, and an elderly woman appears. She looks at him suspiciously, shuffles forward and asks what he wants.

"Glass of beer, please," says Stark in a friendly voice. She cleans a glass and starts drawing her beer the proper way. It takes ten minutes, but his beer has a head on it that will last for the next quarter of an hour. A glass of draught beer is better than all the bottled beer in the world.

"Who has the key of the gate in the middle of the square?" he asks.

"My old Aunt Ann. She lives in the house at the corner near the lime tree," she answers, and shuffles slowly away. No curiosity about who he is, what he has come for, or why he is in-terested in the Seat.

He gets up, pays for his beer and goes to find the old aunt—a simple matter, her house is beside the lime tree where he left his bike. He finds her at home, too old and shaky to walk more than twenty yards, her back bent with rheumatism. One solitary brown tooth is left in her sunken mouth, and her nose is sharp in her bony face.

"She looks more like a witch than Pantar looked like a wizard," thinks Stark.

"What do you want?" she asks, just as suspiciously as the inn-keeper.

"I am Stark, from Wiss. Do you keep the key of the Seat?"

His name means nothing to her. Can she read the papers with her old, watery eyes? Who comes round to talk over the news with her, in this backwater?

"I want to go and sit on the Seat!"

The old woman points with her stick to the little steeple, where a few black crows are flying round. "The dogs will drink your blood and the birds will eat your flesh and your bare bones will lie in the sun!"

"Nice prospect," mutters Stark. "Will you please explain that to me?"

The old woman points to the Seat.

"Can you not read?"

"Well yes, something about making your will. Why is the Seat so dangerous?"

"Why do you want to sit on it?"

"Because that is the last thing I have to do to become King of the country."

"You want to be King?" mutters the old one. "That is strange, very strange. Has the time come at last? Come in and I'll tell you more about the Seat."

Inside the little house he gets a foot-stool to sit on, so he is literally sitting at her feet. That way she can see him—with her bent back she can't look up.

"There are many stories about the Seat. Most of them were told to me by my mother, who heard them from her mother, and so on. Whether they are true or not is for you to decide for yourself.

"Long, long ago, when Wiss still had walls around it and noblemen sat on horses, when smiths made armour and serfs fought with sticks, there was a strange, proud, and self-willed King of Katoren, who was said to be skilled in the magic arts. The nobles flattered him to his face, and laughed behind his back—except for two brothers, Count John and Count Gilbert Starking. These brave men opposed the King openly. They, too, knew a little magic, and often outwitted him. The King hated them and tried to kill them.

"This King thought he could do everything better than anyone else. He found fault with the famous master-builders of Wiss Cathedral, and called them good-for-nothings. He himself would create a real work of art, the like of which would not be found anywhere else on earth. It would be built at his Summer Residence, which was right here in Stillwood. He had a large hoarding erected, so that no one could see it before it was finished. Then he invited all the nobles of the country to a grand summer festival. They came from far and wide, each with his retinue. Never before had such wealth been gathered together in the one place.

"The fourth day of the festival was to culminate in the unveiling ceremony. All the guests gathered round in a wide circle. At a sign from the King, the hoarding was pulled away—and there stood that bulky, shapeless object we know as the Stone Seat.

"The guests showed their admiration in many 'Oh's' and Ah's', which they had rehearsed well before coming. All but two, that is, the brother Counts John and Gilbert. They laughed till the tears ran down their cheeks; they couldn't stop. They pointed to the work of art and laughed louder than ever, and everyone round them started laughing too. All but the King, who went purple with rage. He strode up to the Seat, sat down and looked menacingly at the crowd. Immediately the laughter stopped and an ominous silence fell.

" 'Laugh away, ignoramuses!' cried the King. 'You know not what you laugh at. But I'll tell you this much:

Whoever climbs the seat is sure to die;
So give away your goods and don't ask why.

This is true for everybody, except the King.'

" 'Do you really mean that you will kill anyone who climbs this peculiar heap of stones?' Count John Starking asked.

" 'I will not kill him, but he will surely die.'

" 'This I must try, my King.'

" 'As you will, Count John.' The King rose from the Seat and bowed mockingly to the Count, by way of invitation. Count John walked up, turned, and sat down triumphantly. He smiled to the people and opened his mouth to speak. At that very moment he clutched his heart, grimacing as if in violent pain, and fell to the ground, dead. While everyone still stood looking, Count Gilbert ran to his brother and bent over him. He was indeed dead. Count Gilbert straightened up, and standing there proudly, looked the King straight in the eyes.

" 'Murderer!' he said. 'May the evil spirits possess you!' He walked up to his retinue of servants, picked out the six strongest and heaviest, and beckoned them to follow him to the Seat. Everyone looked on in silence.

" 'I'll take away this curse,' he said. 'After that it will be no more than the ugliest object in all Katoren, made by the most foolish man in the world. Heave me on to the chair.' And while the six men bore him up, he said:

'*Six weighty persons*
On the Stone Seat me lift,
Nothing will happen to me,
The spell is broken, swift.'

"For a few seconds he sat there on the Seat. Then he, too, grasped his heart and whispered, 'Holy Palonius, weighty persons, important persons. They were servants, not important enough. They had to be more important, more weighty, more than . . .' Death claimed him before he could end his sentence, and he fell to the ground."

"What a weird story," says Stark.

"So your name is Stark?"

"Yes."

"Curious: maybe you are a far-off descendant of those Counts. Perhaps you are the one who will break the curse."

"Do you believe this legend?"

"Just listen, I haven't finished yet. There are many more stories about the Seat. In 1602 or 1603 a soldier sat on it. He'd only been sitting there a minute when he was killed by lightning. Then there was a very strong farmer who boasted that he wasn't afraid of anything. He made a bet with his friend and sat on the Seat. A whirlwind blew away half the village, including the boastful farmer. They found him three miles from here, dead."

"Do you really believe all that?"

"Who knows what to believe? Here in the village we think that what Count Starking meant to say was, 'The curse is broken when someone is lifted on to the seat by six people more important than himself'. But let me tell you what I saw myself."

She is silent for a moment, tired after her long story. She collects her thoughts and continues.

"It was about fifty years ago. A group of history students from Wiss came to make a study of Stillwood, to find if it really had been the Summer Residence of the ancient Kings of Katoren. It was a much bigger place in those days, of course. They were a gay, noisy lot, about your age, perhaps a bit older. They wanted to know all about the Seat, naturally, and came to get the stories from my mother. They laughed, a little nervously, and boasted that they did not believe in the curse. Then one of them, a cheerful boy with curly hair, said to my mother, 'Give me the key, old woman, I'll climb into the seat.' 'Be careful, my boy,' she said. They all went off together, a little subdued. The boy with the curls opened the gate and, looking rather tense, jumped up into the Seat. Nothing happened. They all started shouting 'Hurrah, King Peter', and threw their caps high into the air. Peter stood and threw his cap up too, and tried to catch it with his head. The cap came down slightly behind the Seat. He bent over a bit too far, and fell off and broke his neck. Dead, he was."

"Good heavens!" says Stark, deeply impressed.

"There is one more thing to tell," she continues. "Thirty years ago the old King came to Stillwood. He heard the story, had the key brought to him, climbed the seat—and nothing happened."

"But he was a King."

"Exactly, he was a King."

"Did anyone ever try to get himself hoisted into the Seat by six important people?"

"Strange as it may seem, no one has managed to get six important people together. Important people don't like to help less-important people to rise above them."

"Yes, thinking of six very highly-placed people I know, I see the difficulty," says Stark.

He tries to get more information, but she only repeats herself. So he thanks her warmly and says that he will come back soon. It is late in the afternoon when he starts the journey home, and he has to hurry to be back before dark. Uncle Gervaas's bike has no lights.

"They will never do it," says Uncle Gervaas. "They'll never do such a thing. Think of Sure lifting you up! Or Minister Kleen. He'd be afraid he'd catch a contagious disease."

"I don't think they'll do it either, but it's worth asking."

On Saturday night Stark has told Gervaas the whole story. Gervaas is delighted that the last task is so near Wiss. Perhaps he can even lend a hand—but that is looking too far ahead. He shakes his head again and repeats, "They'll never do it."

"Let's give them the chance."

All Sunday he is busy writing a letter to the Ministers. He explains the legends of the Stone Seat in detail, then asks the Ministers, very politely, if they are prepared to lift him into it . . . "If not, I'll try myself, but one never knows with those old tales. With best wishes for your health, yours sincerely, Stark."

The letter is sent off, and all he can do is wait. Uncle Gervaas is very nervous. This time he does not manage to hide himself in the cupboard to hear what is said—fortunately for him, since the Ministers stay in conference for two days and two nights. But he does just "happen" to be cleaning windows all day long in the corridor outside the Council chamber. Scraps of conversation drift out. Minister Watch forgets about his work schedule. Minister Sure laughs—a sour laugh. Minister Strait suppresses the truth, Minister Rush seems quite apathetic. Minister Good scolds his colleagues and Minister Kleen forgets to wash his hands. Finally at the end of forty-eight hours, they send a reply to Stark, and stagger home to bed.

"After ample thought, we see no necessity to comply with your request." It is signed by all the Ministers.

Gervaas is down in the dumps, though he had expected nothing more; but Stark doesn't mind at all. He whistles for his dog. "What a chance they've missed. Now they will never be my Ministers. They have only themselves to blame." He leaves the house contentedly, in the sure knowledge that he will soon be King.

Stark walks through Wiss, buys a few stamps, waves to the people he meets and goes into the Press Club. The journalists there all want to know how he is getting on with his last task.

"Marvellously well," he says. "I've been to Stillwood and checked that the Seat is really solid. I'll, let me see, I'll sit in it to-morrow week, 15 November, at 12 o'clock sharp."

He strolls back home. Uncle Gervaas is on duty at the Palace, which gives Stark the opportunity to write a whole bunch of letters. The first one is to Kim. He asks how the maths is going, when the holidays start, and if they can spend them together, "because I'd be telling a lie if I said I don't like your company." Then he writes to her parents, to thank them for the pillows and the apple pies, and for the charcoal and saltpetre they sent to Smog. He tells them about his other tasks, and how the Ministers have refused to lift him into the Stone Seat, so he is just going to sit on it without them. They must get the fireworks ready for that day.

Then he writes to all the other Mayors, thanking them all for their hospitality and kindness. He asks after the wife and children of the Mayor of Ecumene. Has the big church been a success? How is the new town hall getting on, and the Mayor's own house? He asks the Mayor of Smog if they are all getting nice and sunburned. He tells them all about his seventh task and about 15 November. By the time Gervaas comes home Stark has cramp in his fingers. He takes the letters to the post and spends the evening playing dominoes with his uncle.

Next morning the headlines give the news about 15 November. Nearly every paper mentions the legend of the Seat—the old auntie has had a lot of visitors. The *Katoren Herald* suggests that the Ministers should lift Stark into the Seat, "but when we asked at the Palace about this we were told, 'No comment'." Gervaas beseeches his nephew not to sit in the Seat by himself.

"Just wait and see," says Stark, untroubled. "I'll be all right."

The following week uncle is a bundle of nerves and nephew as calm as a lake in the woods. He refuses to worry about a thing. On Wednesday night, in the middle of a game of dominoes, Stark goes to answer a ring of the door-bell. There stand Kim and her father. Kim rushes into his arms, and not until she has kissed him a dozen times does her father get a chance to shake hands.

"Do come in," says Stark. "You are welcome."

Gervaas and Kim's father get acquainted. The dominoes go back in their box and Kim disappears into the kitchen to make coffee.

"Aren't you surprised to see us?" asks the Mayor of Powdermill.

"No, not in the least, I was expecting you. I know you are a noble and faithful man."

"Well, well, and we thought we would surprise you."

"It was a surprise to see Kim," says Stark quickly, "I hadn't hoped for that."

"Is it too much to ask you to explain what all this is about?" says Uncle Gervaas. "I don't know what's going on."

"You see, Gervaas, Stark wrote to us about the Ministers refusing to lift him into the Stone Seat. Now I'm not all that important a person, but still, my position is slightly higher than Stark's—till Friday, that is—and I want to give him a hand to climb into that cursed Seat."

"That is mighty good of you, sir," says Gervaas, "but you know we need six . . ."

The bell rings.

". . . six important . . ."

"It isn't Friday yet, Uncle," says Stark. "Let's see who's ringing the bell so late at night."

The Mayor of Decibel is shown in. He embraces Stark and immediately starts talking—he is very good at that. It turns out that he has come for the same purpose as the Mayor of Powdermill. Next day, Thursday, the Mayor of Ecumene arrives in the morning, and in the afternoon the Mayor of Swindelburg, with his wife—two return tickets! What a terrific expense for them!

"The piano can wait," he says. "My wife was so eager to come too."

Kim's father asks how they will get to Stillwood tomorrow. Stark has not thought about that. There is no train or bus service.

"You had better appoint a Minister of Transport on Saturday," the Mayor of Powdermill teases him. "You don't seem to have that department very well organized. Leave it to me."

He is lucky to find an old bus for hire in the town. Everything else that moves has already been booked by people planning to go to Stillwood the next morning.

That night Gervaas comes home saying, "I have taken the day off tomorrow."

Stark puts his arm round the aged shoulders. "My dear, good old Uncle, from tomorrow all your days will be days off!"

"There are only four Mayors, two too few," remarks Gervaas. "Never mind, I don't expect you'll die with four of them. You might break two legs."

Stark bursts out laughing. "Then you'll have to push me in a wheelbarrow."

The Mayor of Decibel has brought six bottles of wine, so they all have an exceedingly cheerful evening in Uncle Gervaas's little house. The gaiety reaches its height when the bell rings, and in comes the Mayor of Equilibrium.

"Only one broken leg; now you can walk on crutches," giggles Gervaas. "Thanks for coming, madam. Now I won't have to push him."

Kim doesn't like that sort of joke. Moreover she is not so sure that all will be well.

"Stark," she whispers, "the old aunt said six, not five. Five could be as dangerous as none. Where is the Mayor of Smog?"

"Don't fuss, darling. Everything will be all right."

King of Katoren

At eleven o'clock Kim's father drives up to the front door in his shaky little bus, and they all get in—Gervaas, all the Mayors, the Mayor of Swindelburg's wife, and of course, Kim and Stark. Just as they are about to start, a shining Rolls Royce comes round the corner. A chauffeur gets out and opens the door, and there, much to the delight of the nine people in the bus, is the Mayor of Smog.

"Wait a minute!" calls Stark. He jumps out of the bus and greets his rich friend.

"Can I do anything for you?" the millionaire asks.

"You've arrived just at the right moment. Your five colleagues are about to start for Stillwood."

"All right, I'll follow you."

At that moment the Mayor of Decibel puts his head out of the window and yells, "Come in here, old man, much nicer!" Mr Smog looks sceptical, then smiles, saying, "Right you are. I'm getting poorer every minute with all this sunshine in my town."

So, after all, Stark has his six important people all together: the talkative Mayor of Decibel, the energetic Mayor of Powdermill, the elegant Mayor of Smog, the pious Mayor of Ecumene, the modest Mayor of Swindelburg, and the sober Mayor of Equilibrium.

Kim is content now. She sits quietly at the back of the bus, looking happy. They all drive off, stopping only once for a flat tyre. Just after midday they arrive at Stillwood.

"Well," remarks Stark, looking at the crowds, "I see Uncle Gervaas is not the only one to take a day off." With some difficulty they reach the house beside the lime tree, where the old aunt stands waiting, the key in her apron pocket.

Then to the Seat. As Stark fumbles with the lock, the people suddenly make room for . . . six Ministers in two rows of three.

Their black coats make a sombre contrast to the gay crowd. They stand right at the front.

Meantime Stark has opened the gate and he and his six friends walk through it. Silence falls. The five men hoist Stark up, and the Mayor of Equilibrium takes hold of the end of his coat. "One, two, three . . . hup!" Kim's father calls out, the leader as always. There sits Stark. The stone is cold and hard, but who minds?

Dead silence. Will he drop dead? The people wait. Then Stark thumbs his nose at the Ministers and everyone starts to cheer. Five hundred times the people throw up their arms and shout "Hurrah, hurrah!" after the Mayor of Decibel has shouted "Long Live the King!"

At the two hundred and first time, the lips of Minister Good begin to tremble. At the two hundred and fiftieth time, one arm of Minister Rush is slightly raised. At the three hundredth time, none of the Ministers can keep still any longer, and they begin to murmur. At the three hundred and fiftieth time, they all lift their arms half-way to their ears. By the last hundred times they act just like the rest of the people, and raise their arms and cheer.

After that they all start back for Wiss. The village innkeeper is sorry to see them go—in spite of all the noise, which she hates, she has drawn more beer that one morning than in all the past ten years.

"Your Majesty," says Minister Sure, "may we offer you our cars?"

Stark grins, but prefers to go in the shaky old bus with Kim, Gervaas, and the Mayors.

"We'll meet at St Aloysius," he says.

There in the old Cathedral, in a crystal case, lies the crown of the old King. Minister Sure lifts it and places it on Stark's head.

"As Ministers of this country, we declare and confirm, that you, by the wish of the people, according to the rules that we stipulated, and in all righteousness saw fulfilled, are now proclaimed King of Katoren."

"Well said!" says Stark. "I hope it doesn't hurt too much to see the crown on my head instead of on your own; but just think, it would hide your beautiful hair."

He goes and stands on a chair.

"My people," he calls out, "thank you for your help and support. I have a few things to say, now. The first is, that every year I mean to set myself one task like the seven I have just fulfilled. If ever I fail in one I will no longer be King. Secondly, the Mayor of Powdermill will phone his town in a minute and have crates of fireworks dispatched to all parts of the country. These fireworks were produced during my stay in Powdermill, so they are all ready to go. We are going to feast for three days—we have a lot of feasting to catch up with. We'll make up for lost time by giving fewer speeches. So, thirdly, this is the longest speech I'll ever make. Joy and good fortune to you all!"

Then the festivities begin, and the people of Katoren show the whole world how to run a celebration. When all the thousands of different sorts of fireworks are extinguished, Stark goes to the Palace to rule his country.

The Mayors come to the Palace to take their leave.

"May I suggest something to you?" says Stark. "I don't believe in Ministries of Honesty, Diligence, and what not. Instead I think we should have a Ministry of Health, and I think that the Mayor of Swindelburg would be the right person to organize it."

"Me?" says the little man, taken by surprise.

"You. A Ministry of Fresh Air and Clear Water seems to me the right job for the Mayor of Smog, and a Ministry of Church, Culture and Society for the Mayor of Ecumene. And you, Madam Mayor, would you be so good as to take the Care for Backward Territories on your shoulders? A Ministry of Defence and De-armament seems the right thing for Kim's father, I think, and I should like you, Mayor of Decibel, to take charge of the Ministry that teaches people to listen to each other's points of view—you'll be Minister of Democracy. Your towns will have to elect new Mayors in your place. Do you all agree?"

The Mayors nod cheerfully, and leave to put their affairs in order.

Stark orders the old Ministers to come and see him.

"You can no longer be Ministers," he says, "but you won't be made redundant. I have other work for you." He takes a handful of the letters that have accumulated in the last few months. Each one asks for Stark to come and help them. He reads one.

"Here," he says, "I see there is a lie-well in Chickenroost. That might be just the thing for you, Mr Strait."

Charles Strait bows low and takes the letter.

"The runaway clocks of Timelag. How would that suit you, Mr Watch?"

Sebastian Watch accepts his task.

"Here is something for you, Mr Sure. The burning laughing-gas at Joyhill."

"At your service, Your Majesty," says Henry Sure.

Stark looks through the heap of letters again, and finds the right task for Bonifacius Good: the naughty servants of Fiddle.

And after the former Minister of Virtue has accepted his task, "Here is something for you, Mr Rush: the clotting mercury of Lazidizzibell."

"Thank you," says Tom Rush.

After that, Stark has to search for some time before he finds a task for the last of his old Ministers. At last he finds just the thing. "Mr Kleen, I suggest that you go and tackle the dog-plague at Dirtykerb."

"I'll do my utmost, Your Majesty," promises Philip Kleen.

All six bow low, and leave the Palace to start on their new assignments.

"I've ruled enough for today," says Stark to Kim, who is leaving that night for Powdermill. "Are you looking forward to going home?"

She shakes her head.

"When you've ploughed through all that math and so on, will you come back? We might get married. I don't know anything about math, and it might come in handy to have someone about who did."

She bites his ear and he yells, "Ow!"

"Why do you never say you love me, just ordinary?"

"I love you—extra-ordinary."

We will leave them to their moment of privacy—a rare treat for royalty. For those who are very inquisitive, I can reveal that they eventually do get married and live long and happily ever after.